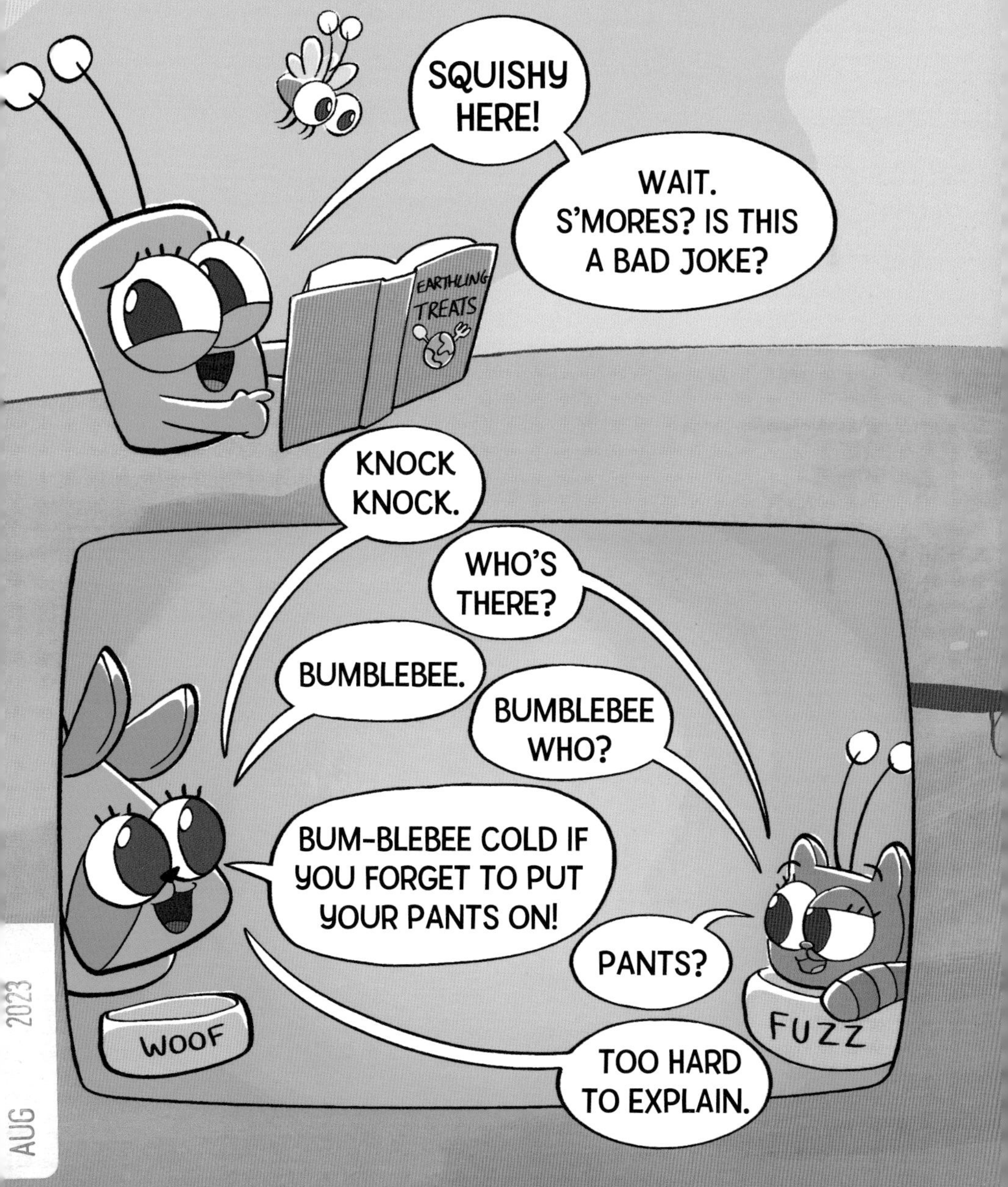
SQUISHY HERE!
WAIT. S'MORES? IS THIS A BAD JOKE?
EARTHLING TREATS
KNOCK KNOCK.
WHO'S THERE?
BUMBLEBEE.
BUMBLEBEE WHO?
BUM-BLEBEE COLD IF YOU FORGET TO PUT YOUR PANTS ON!
PANTS?
WOOF
FUZZ
TOO HARD TO EXPLAIN.

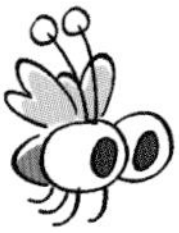

Want to read s'more?

Show and Smell

Museum Sleepover

(Coming in January 2024)

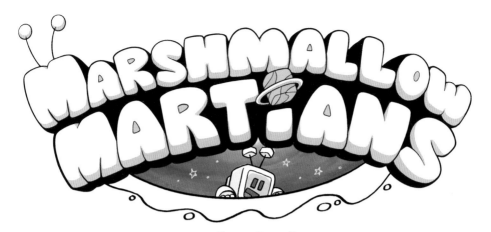

MARSHMALLOW MARTIANS

Earth School

WOW!

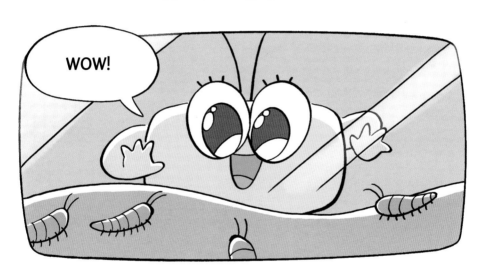

by Deanna Kent
illustrated by Neil Hooson

A STEPPING STONE BOOK™
Random House New York

This book, dear reader, is written especially for *you* with a wish that it reminds you of how wacky and wonderful the world can be. Please write your name here:

____

It takes many fabulous humans to make a Marshmallow Martians book. Among them are Gemma Cooper, Heidi Kilgras, and Michelle Cunningham. Thank you for being part of this squishy adventure. Also, big love to the extraordinary students (and Lori and Sarah!) at the Galiano Community School who inspired us as we wrote this, and to teachers and librarians everywhere—especially Sharon Bede and Sherry Nasedkin.

—D.K. and N.H.

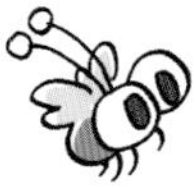

 Published in the United States by Random House Children's Books, a division of Penguin Random House LLC, New York.
Random House and the colophon are registered trademarks and A Stepping Stone Book and the colophon are trademarks of Penguin Random House LLC.
RH Graphic with the book design is a trademark of Penguin Random House LLC.
Visit us on the Web! rhcbooks.com
Educators and librarians, for a variety of teaching tools, visit us at RHTeachersLibrarians.com

Library of Congress Cataloging-in-Publication Data is available upon request.
ISBN 978-0-593-56610-7 (hardcover) — ISBN 978-0-593-56611-4 (library binding)
ISBN 978-0-593-56612-1 (ebook)

MANUFACTURED IN CHINA
10 9 8 7 6 5 4 3 2 1
First Edition

Contents

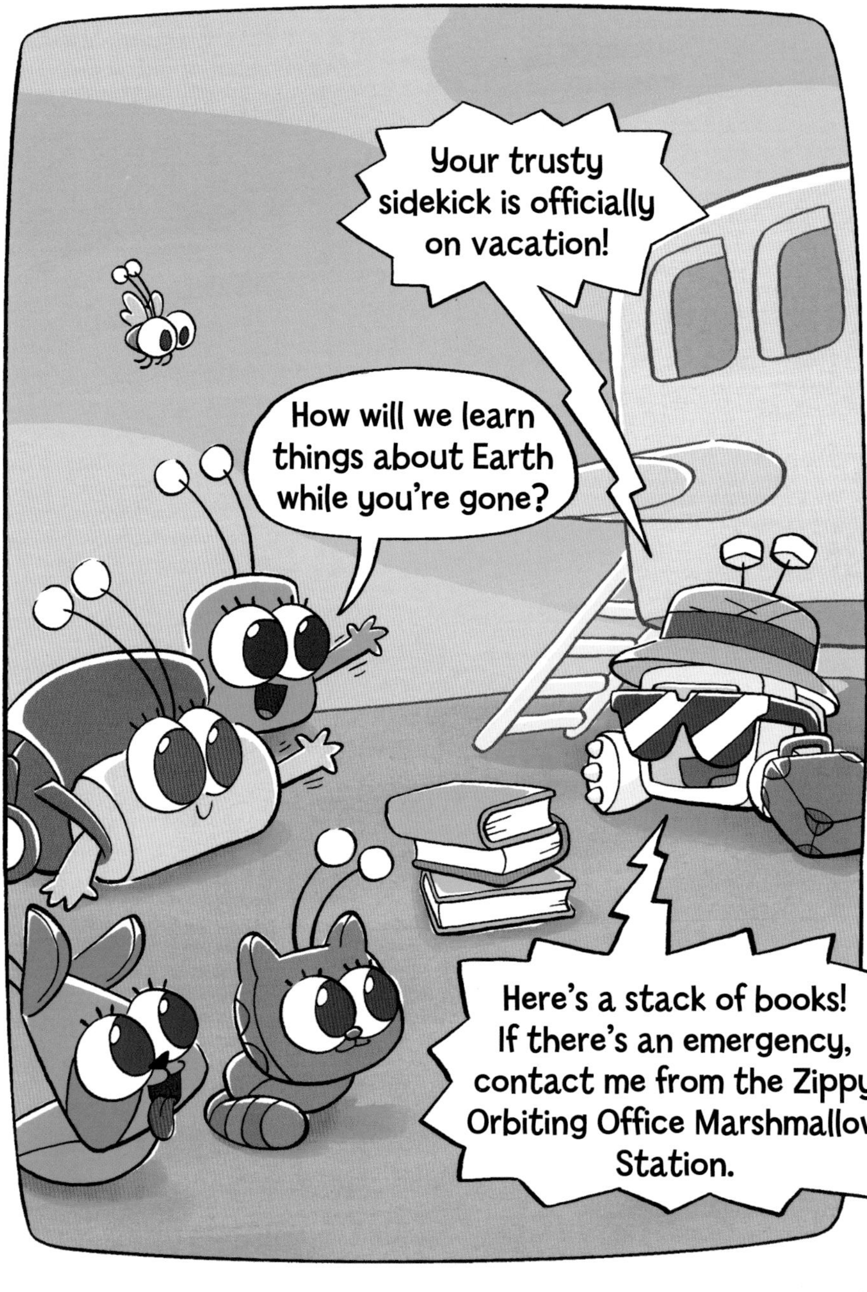
Your trusty sidekick is officially on vacation!
How will we learn things about Earth while you're gone?
Here's a stack of books! If there's an emergency, contact me from the Zippy Orbiting Office Marshmallow Station.

Chapter 1
Bee Curious!

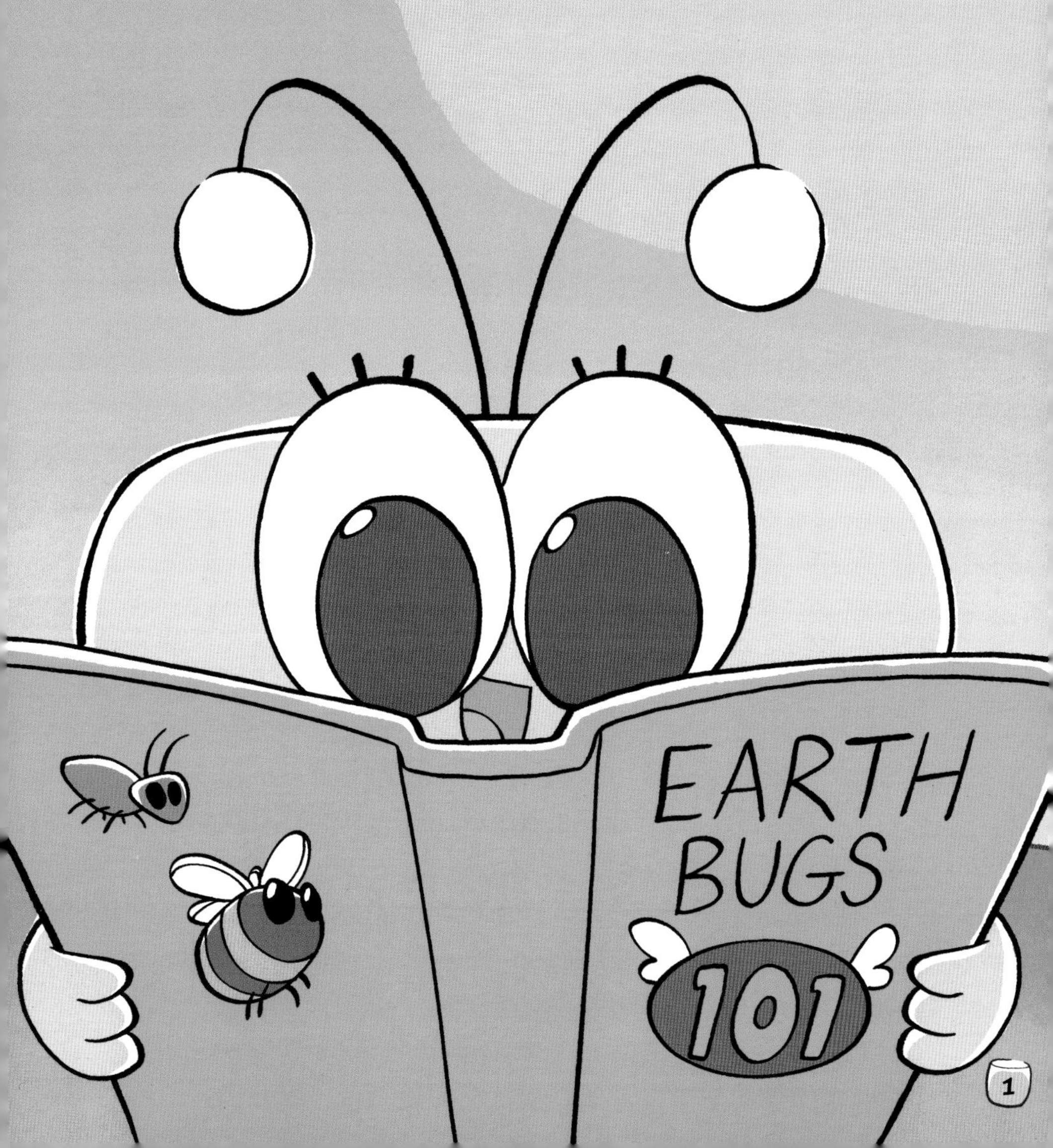
EARTH
BUGS
101

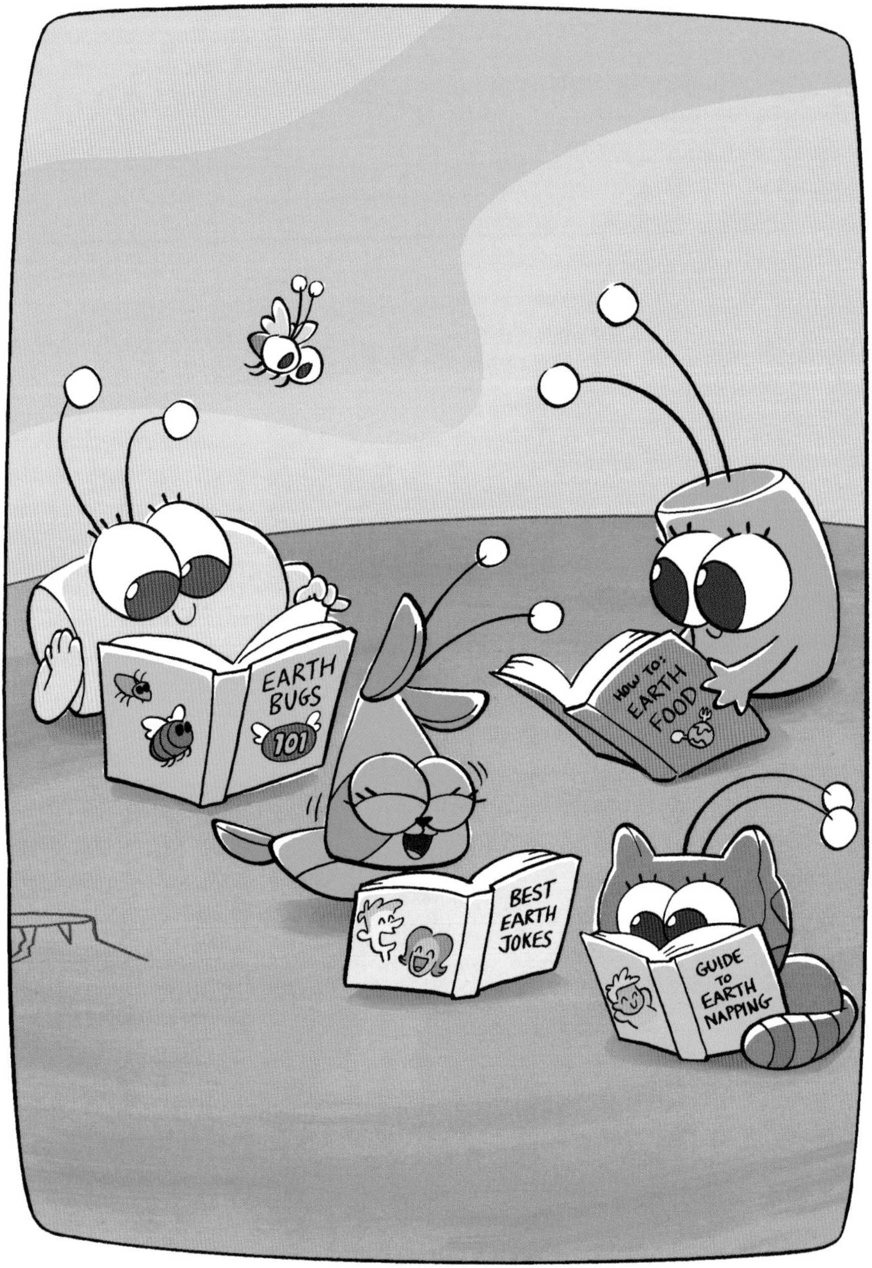
EARTH
BUGS
101
HOW TO:
EARTH
FOOD
BEST
EARTH
JOKES
GUIDE
TO
EARTH
NAPPING

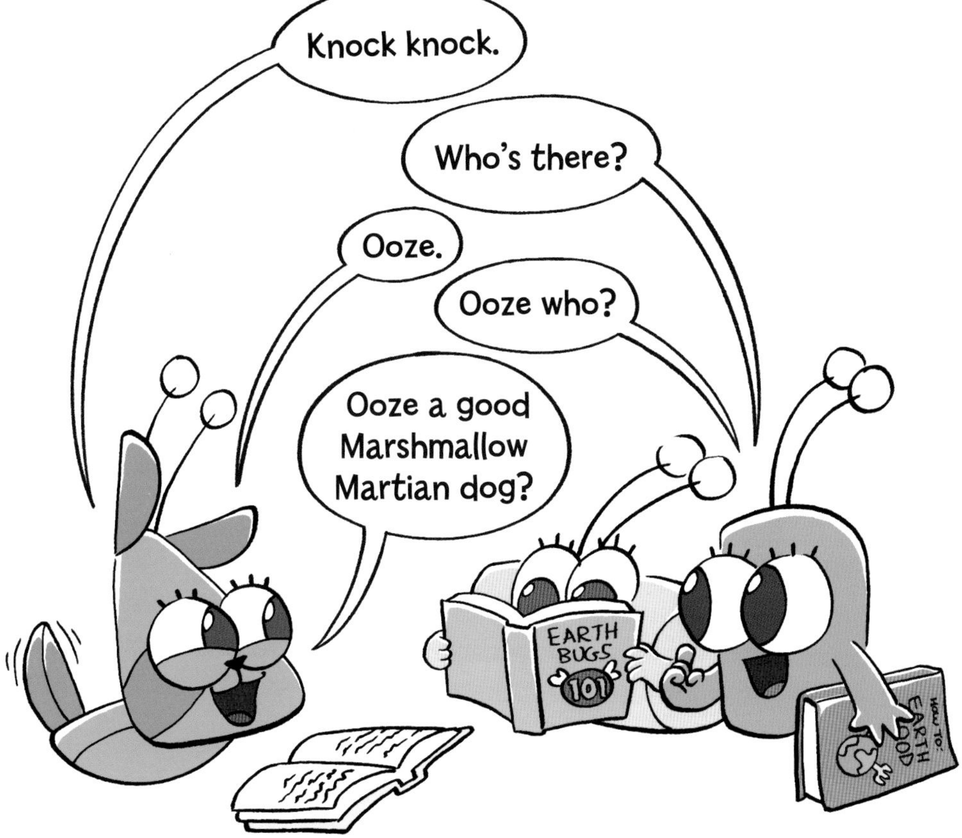
Knock knock.
Who's there?
Ooze.
Ooze who?
Ooze a good Marshmallow Martian dog?
EARTH BUGS 101
HOW TO: EARTH FOOD

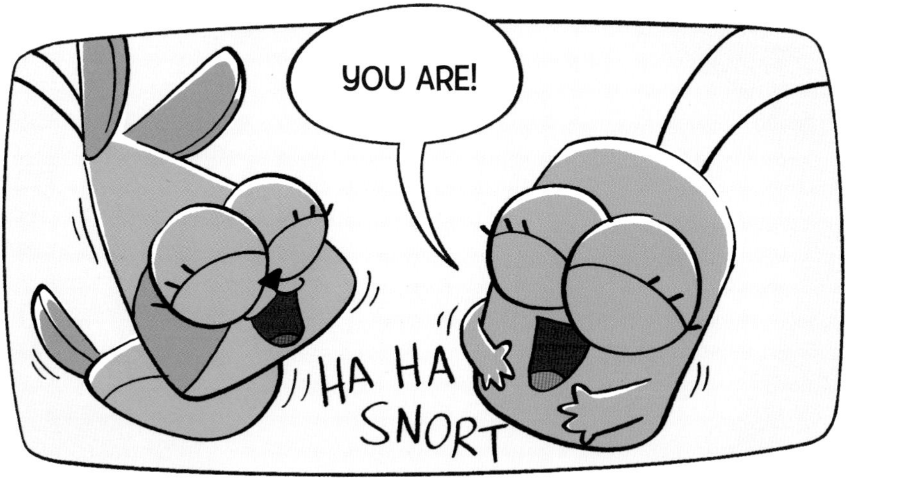
YOU ARE!
HA HA SNORT

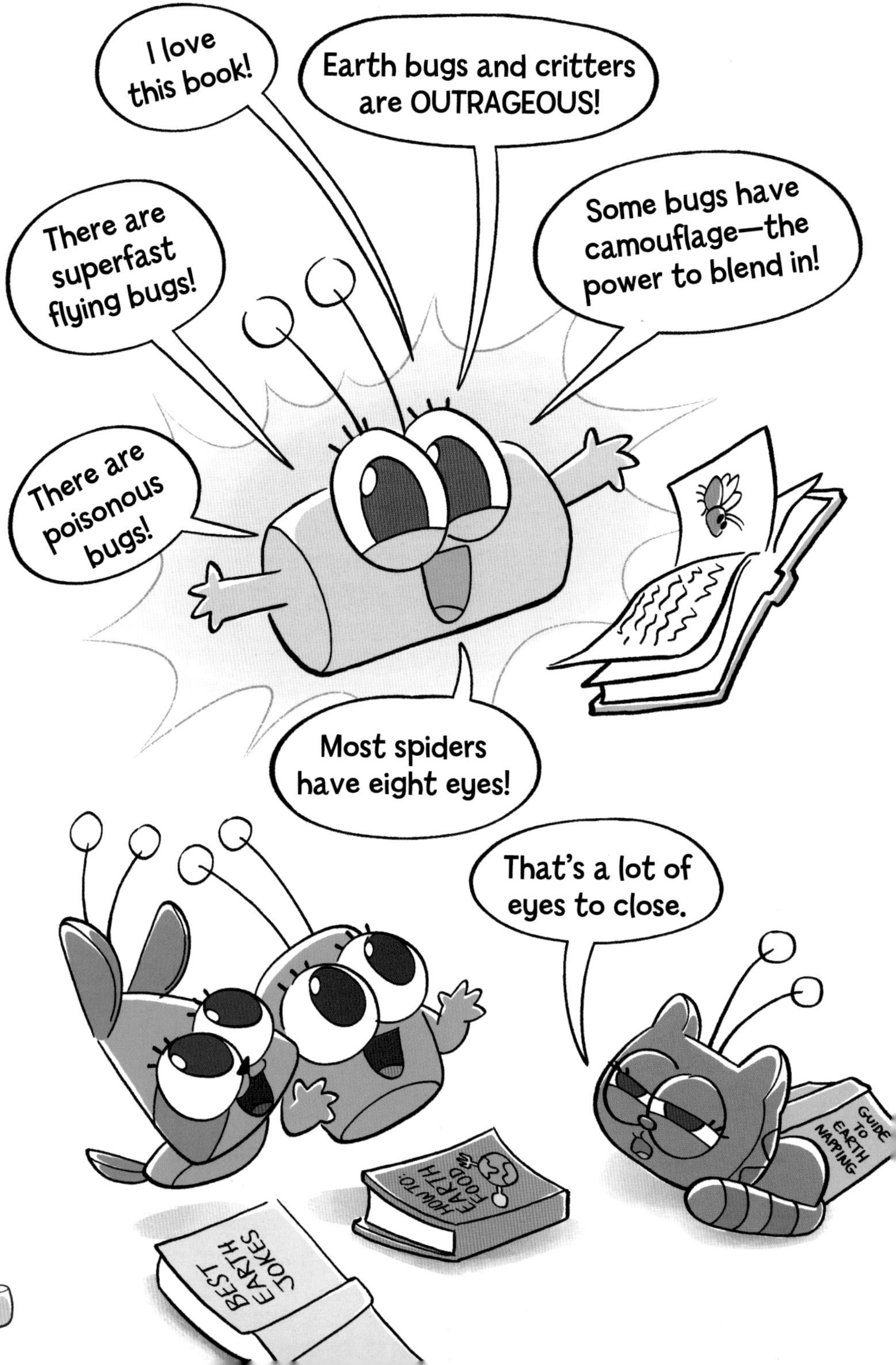
I love this book!
Earth bugs and critters are OUTRAGEOUS!
There are superfast flying bugs!
Some bugs have camouflage—the power to blend in!
There are poisonous bugs!
Most spiders have eight eyes!
That's a lot of eyes to close.
HOW TO: EARTH FOOD
GUIDE TO EARTH NAPPING
BEST EARTH JOKES

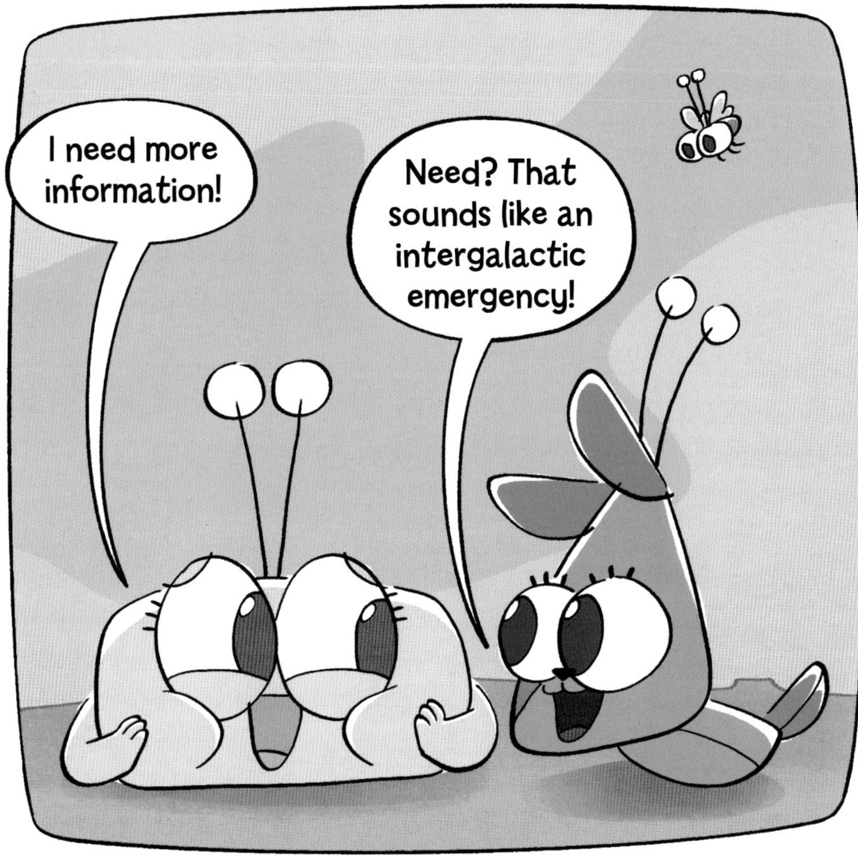
I need more information!
Need? That sounds like an intergalactic emergency!

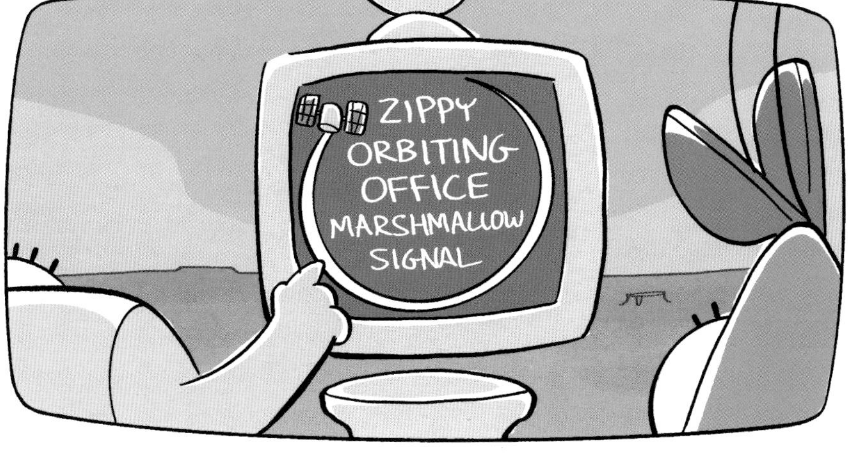
ZIPPY ORBITING OFFICE MARSHMALLOW SIGNAL

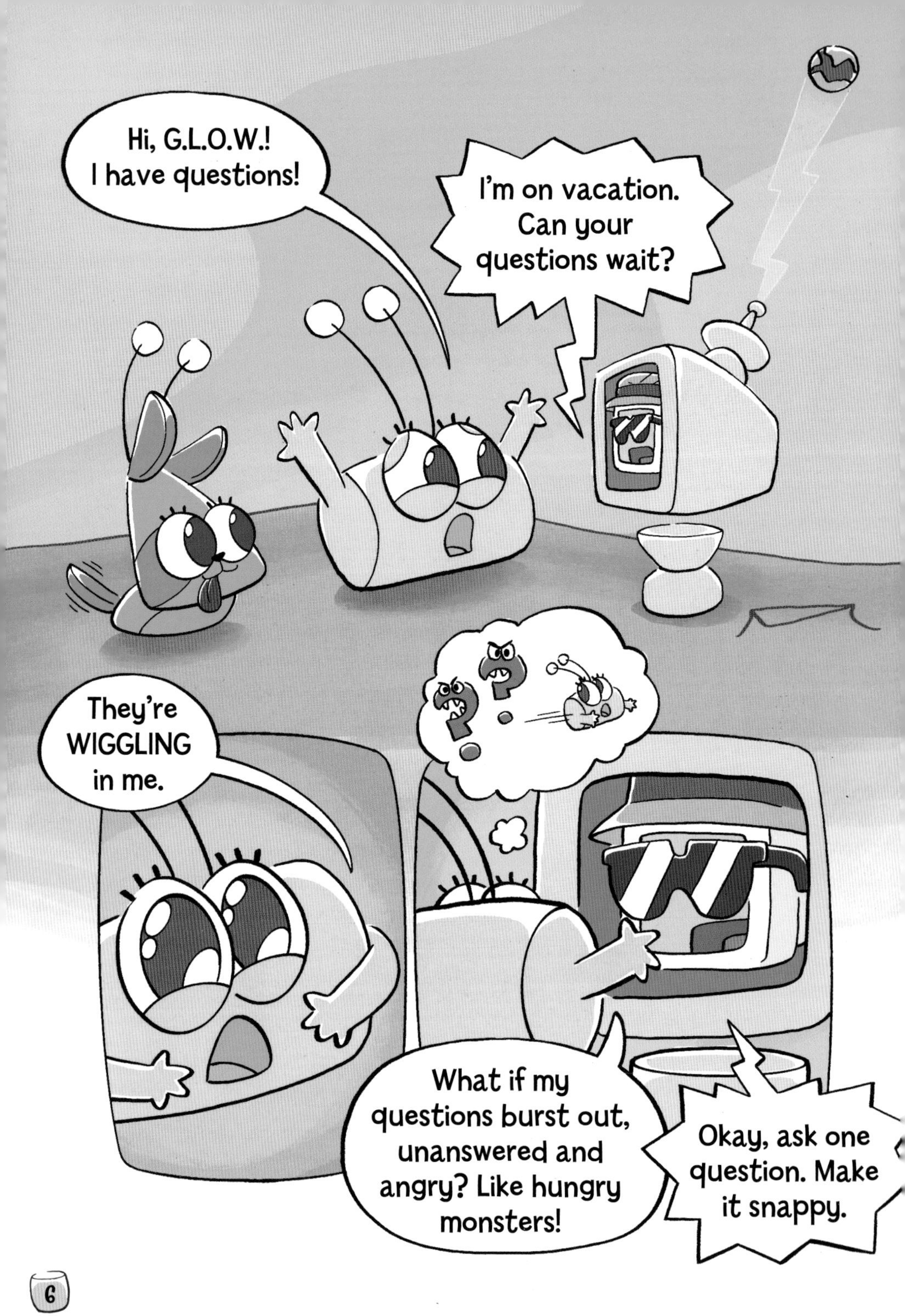
Hi, G.L.O.W.! I have questions!
I'm on vacation. Can your questions wait?
They're WIGGLING in me.
What if my questions burst out, unanswered and angry? Like hungry monsters!
Okay, ask one question. Make it snappy.

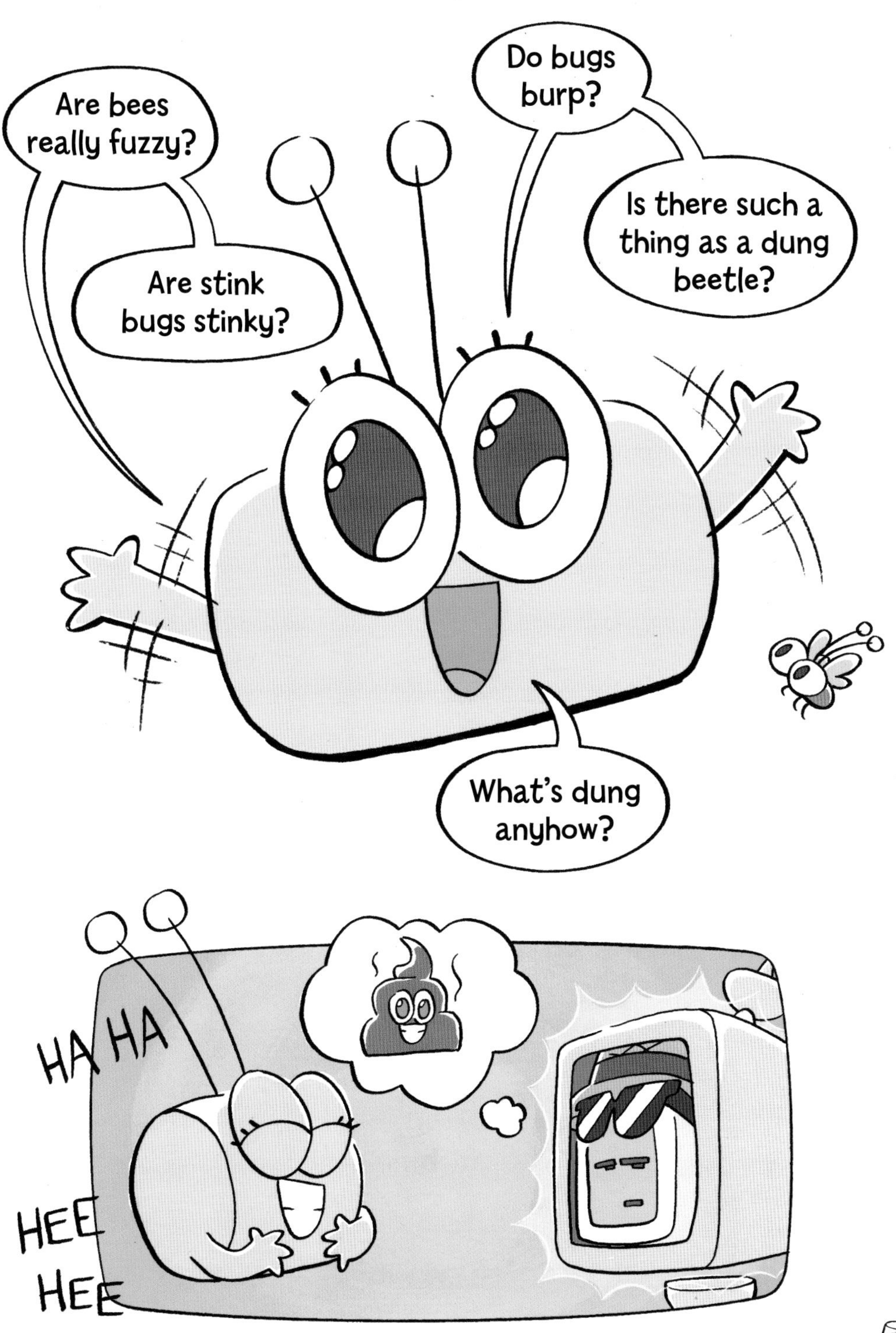

Are bees really fuzzy?
Do bugs burp?
Are stink bugs stinky?
Is there such a thing as a dung beetle?
What's dung anyhow?
HA HA
HEE HEE

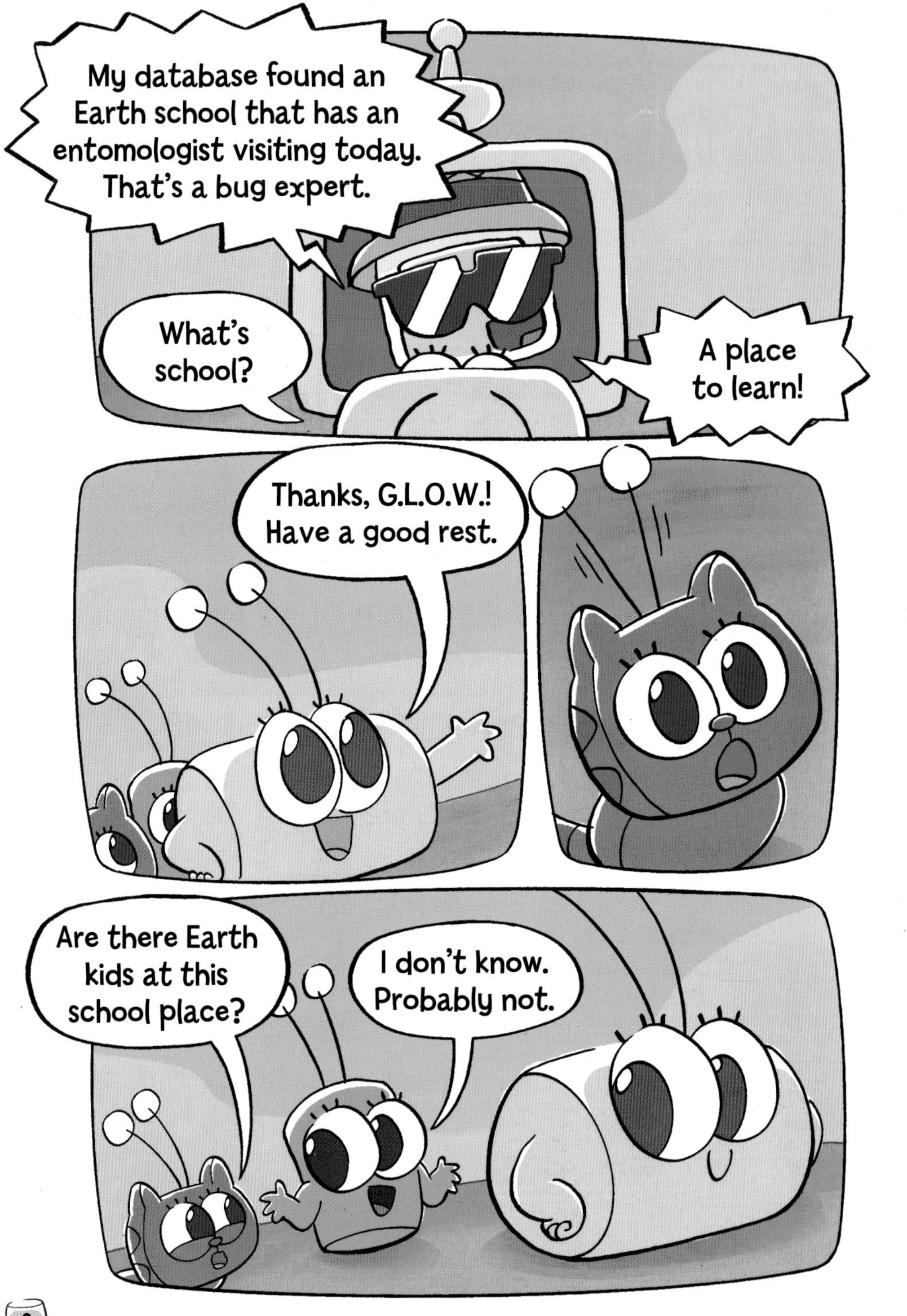
My database found an Earth school that has an entomologist visiting today. That's a bug expert.
What's school?
A place to learn!
Thanks, G.L.O.W.! Have a good rest.
Are there Earth kids at this school place?
I don't know. Probably not.

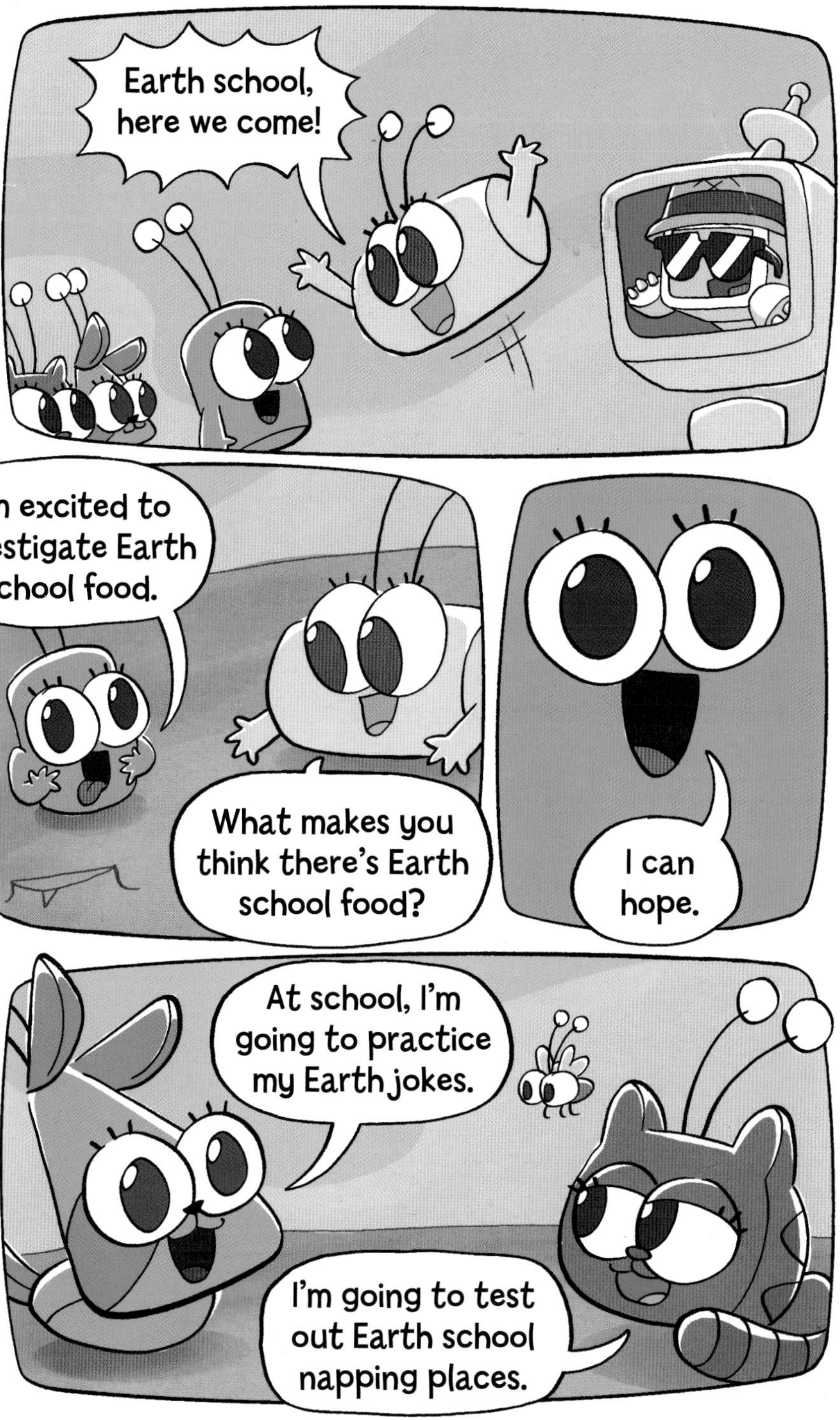
Earth school, here we come!
I'm excited to investigate Earth school food.
What makes you think there's Earth school food?
I can hope.
At school, I'm going to practice my Earth jokes.
I'm going to test out Earth school napping places.

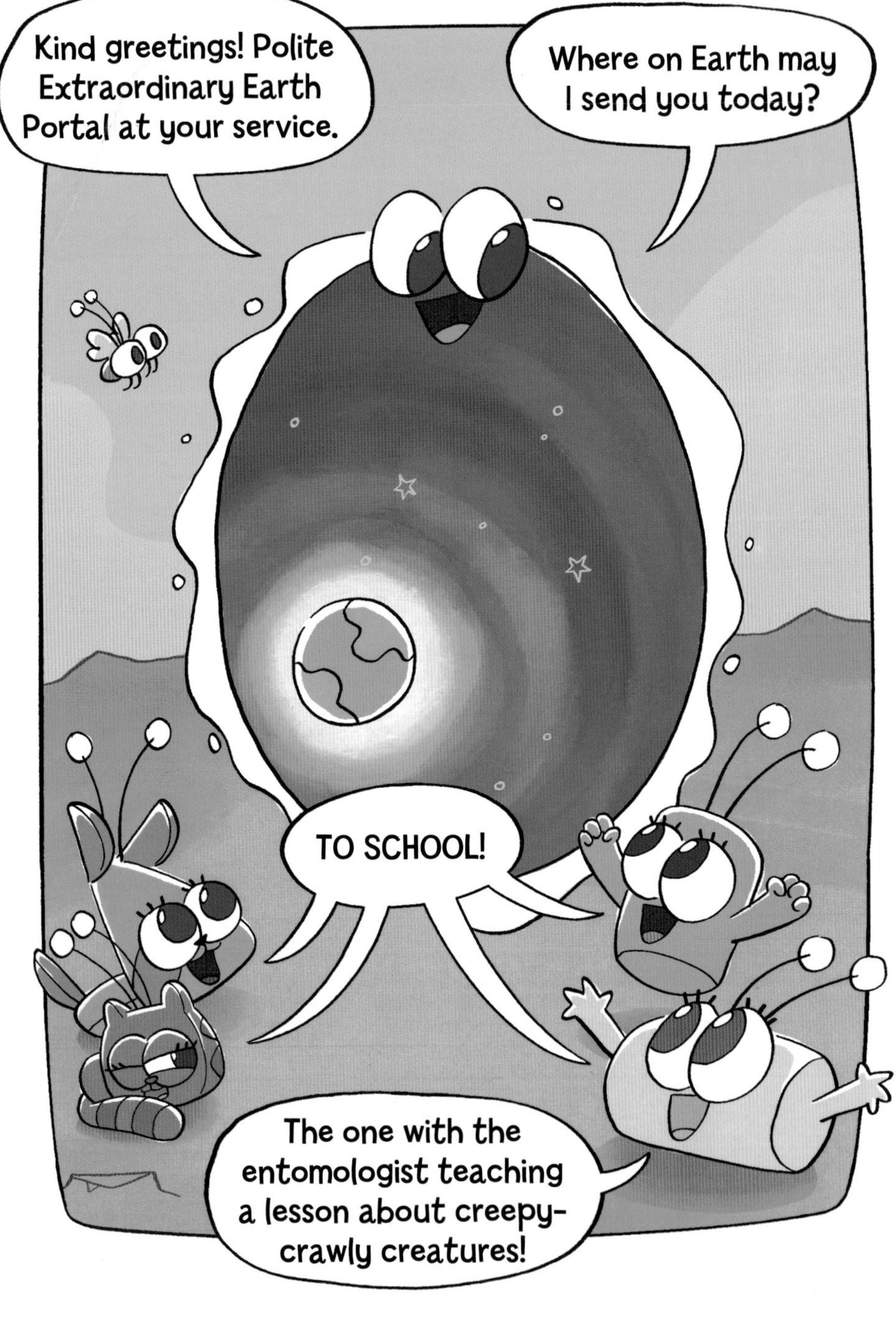
Kind greetings! Polite Extraordinary Earth Portal at your service.
Where on Earth may I send you today?
TO SCHOOL!
The one with the entomologist teaching a lesson about creepy-crawly creatures!

Chapter 2
Snug's Bugs

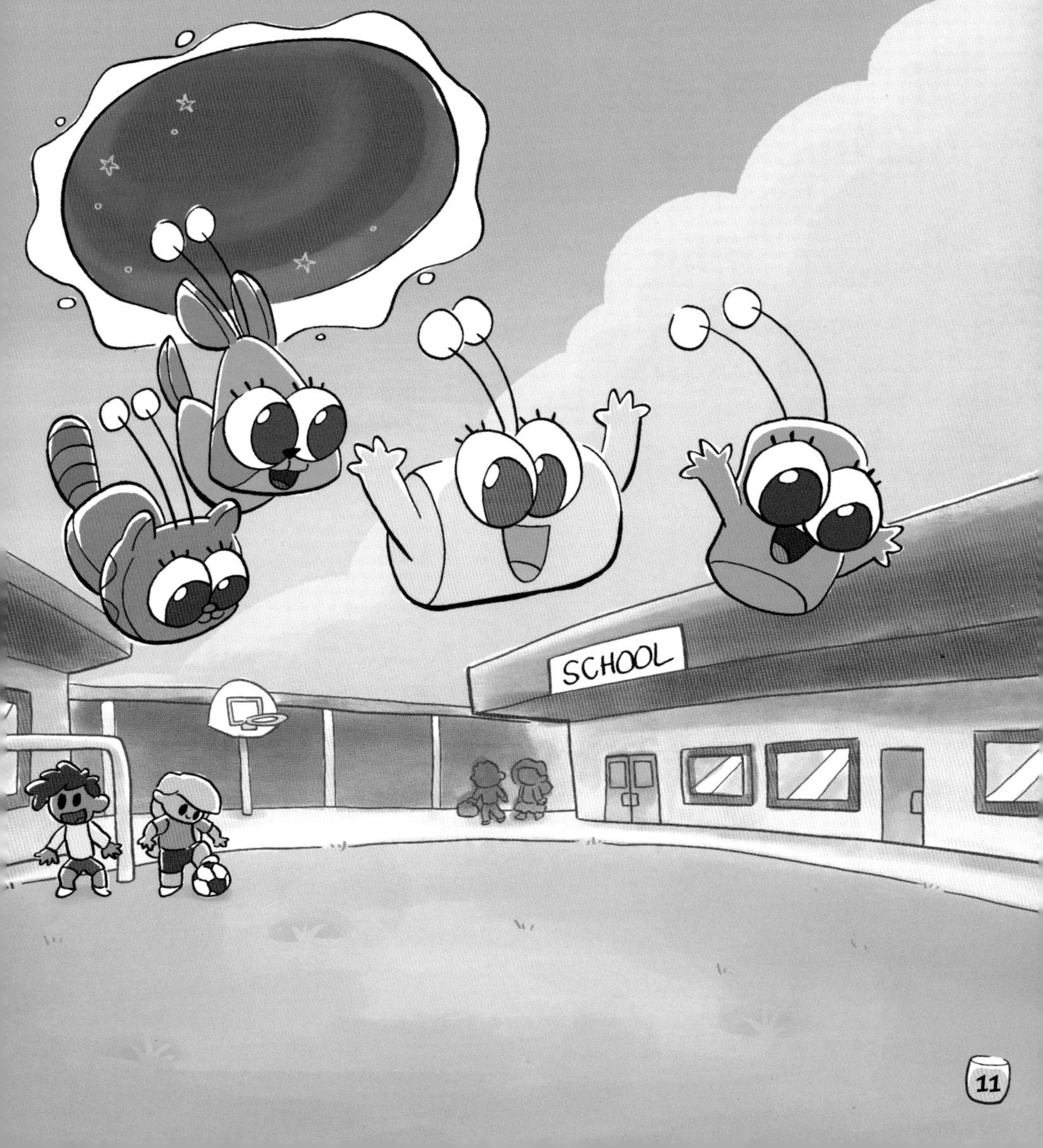
SCHOOL

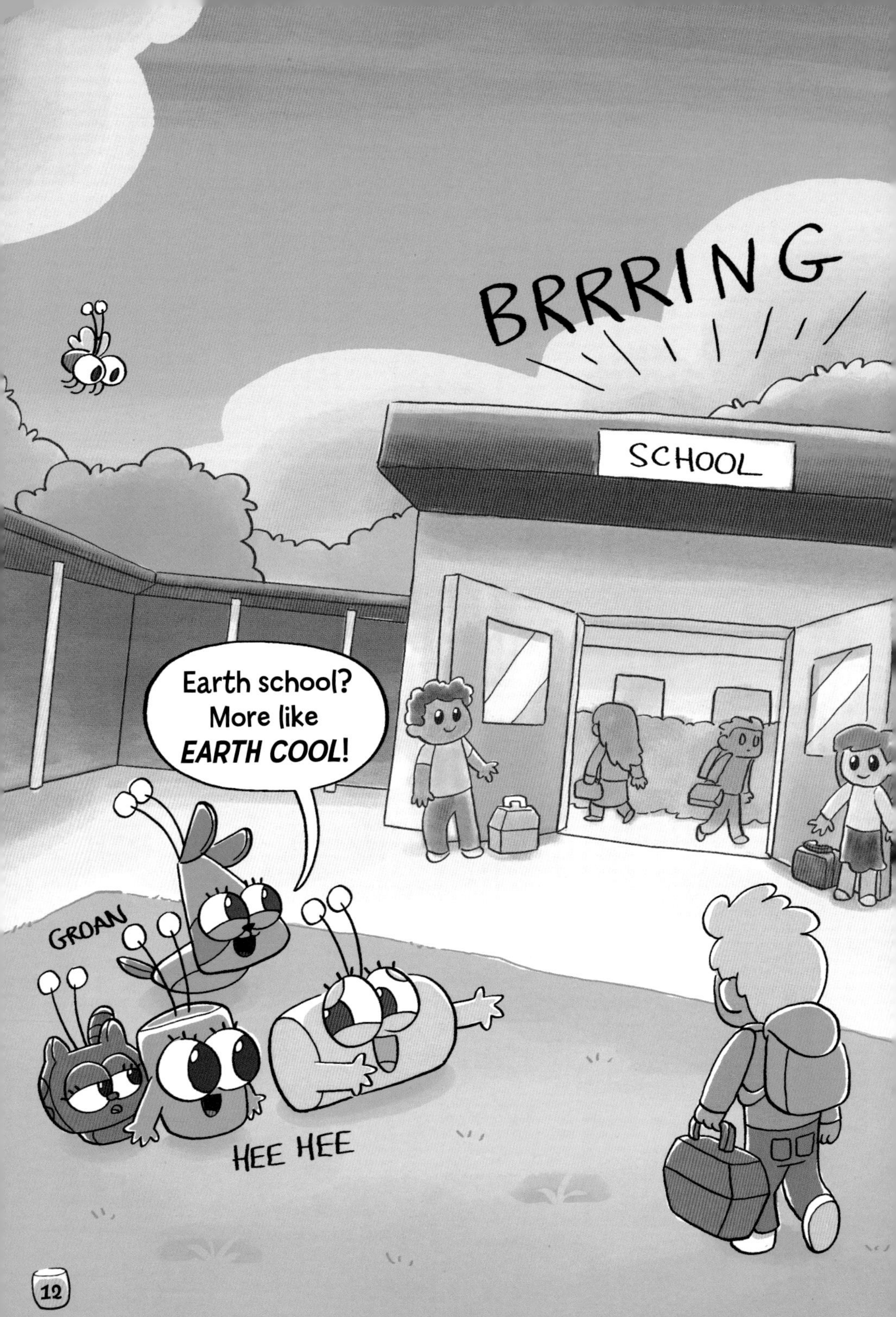
BRRRING
SCHOOL
Earth school? More like *EARTH COOL*!
GROAN
HEE HEE

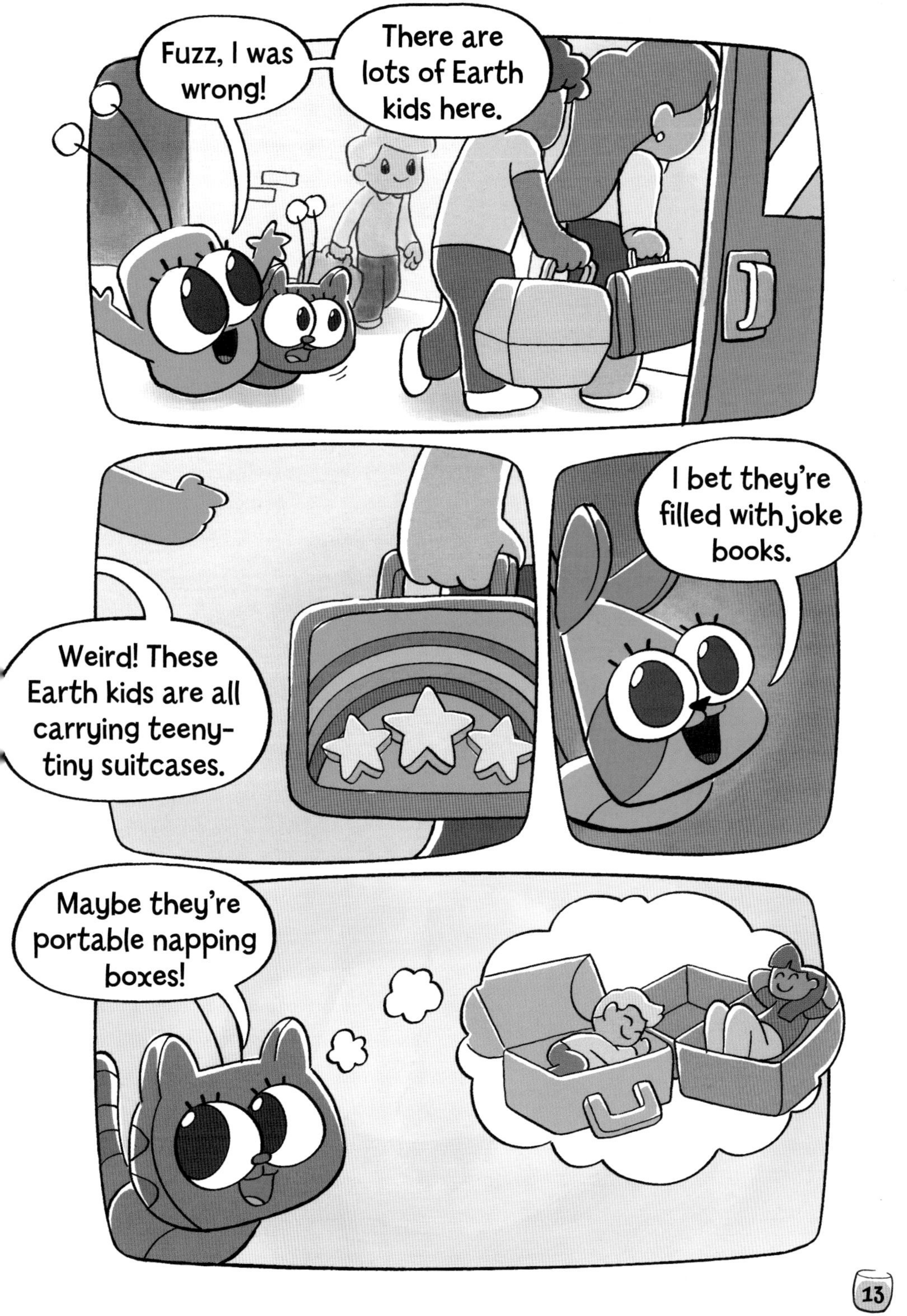
Fuzz, I was wrong!
There are lots of Earth kids here.
Weird! These Earth kids are all carrying teeny-tiny suitcases.
I bet they're filled with joke books.
Maybe they're portable napping boxes!

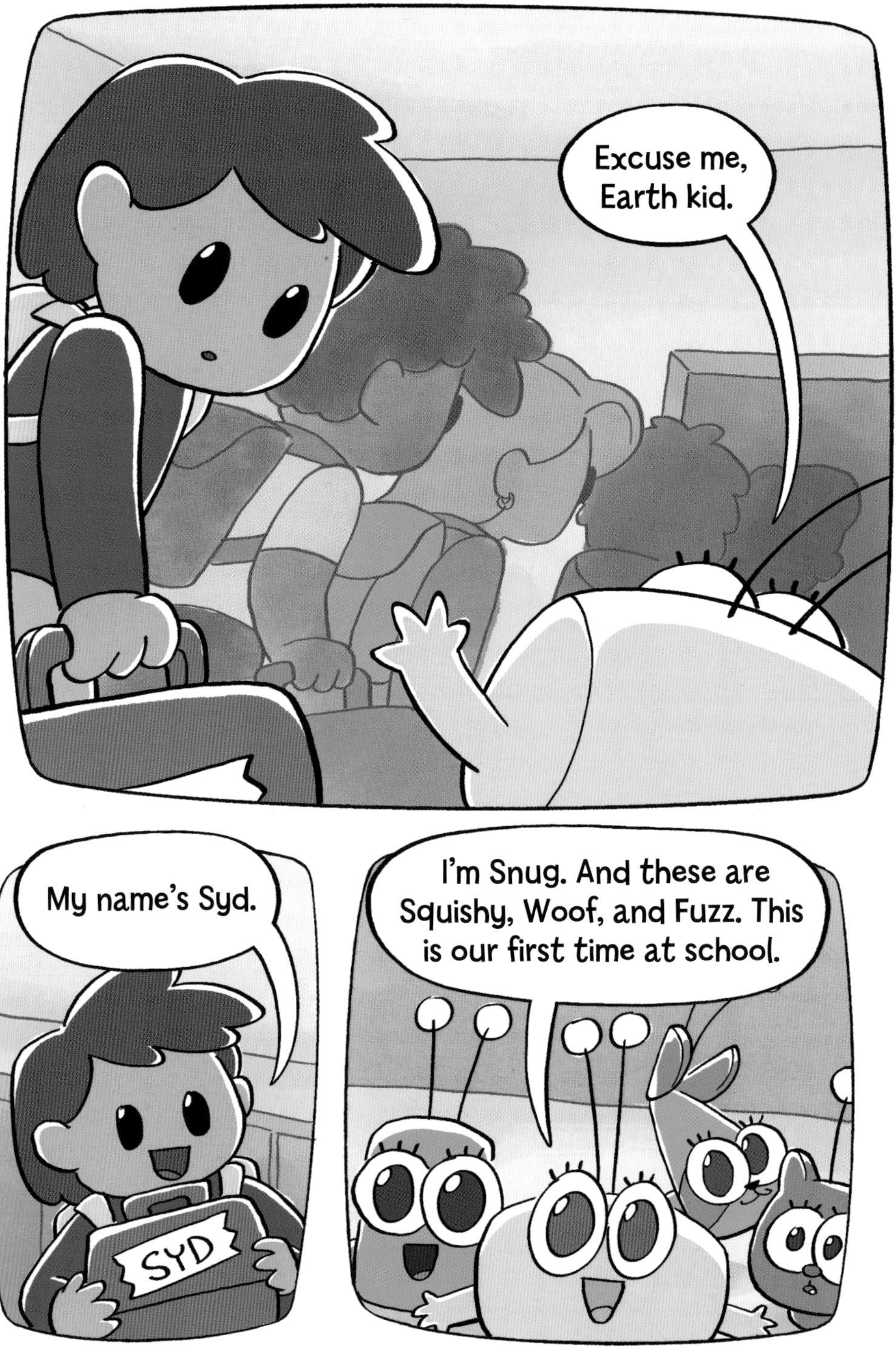
Excuse me, Earth kid.
My name's Syd.
SYD
I'm Snug. And these are Squishy, Woof, and Fuzz. This is our first time at school.

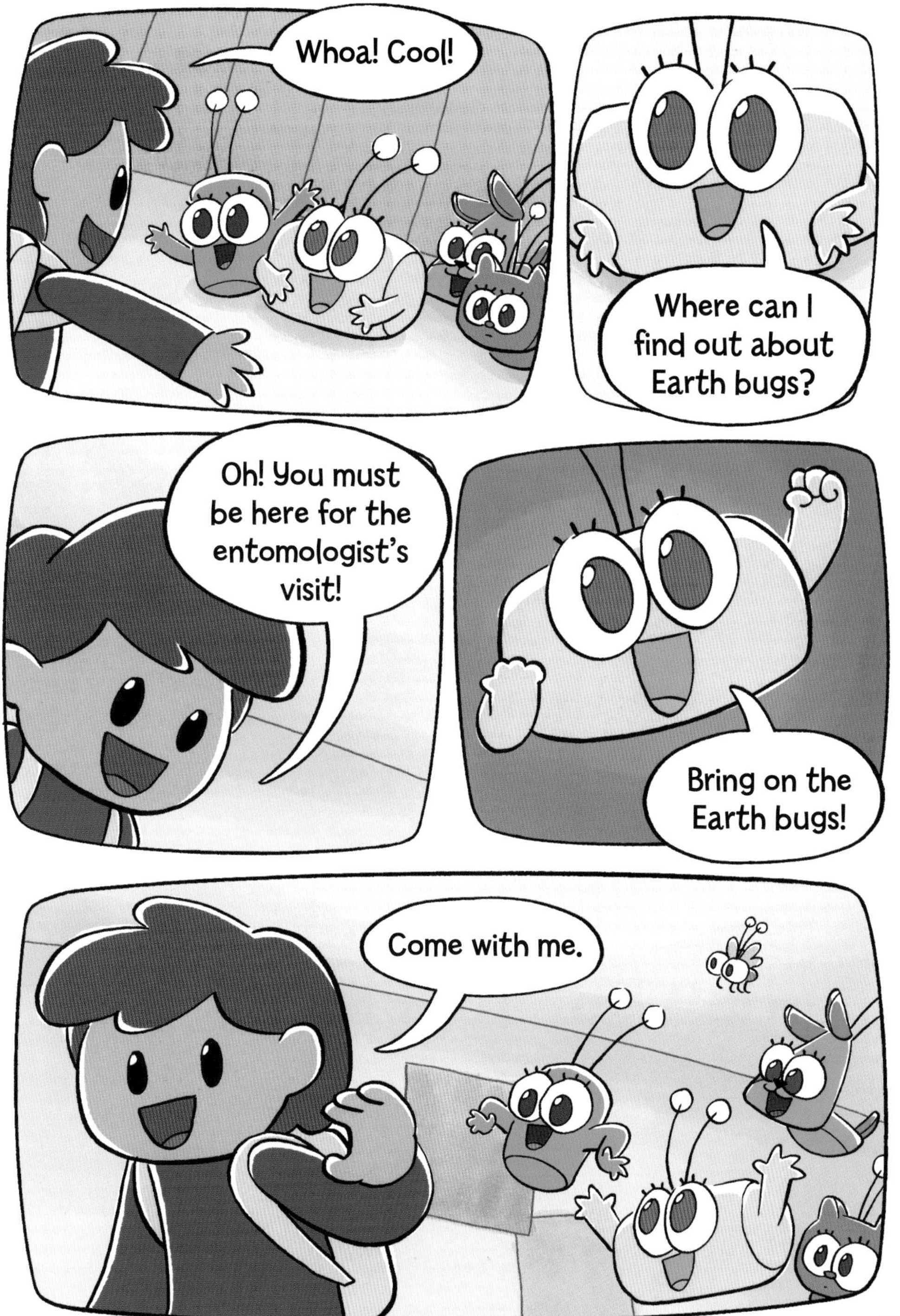
Whoa! Cool!
Where can I find out about Earth bugs?
Oh! You must be here for the entomologist's visit!
Bring on the Earth bugs!
Come with me.

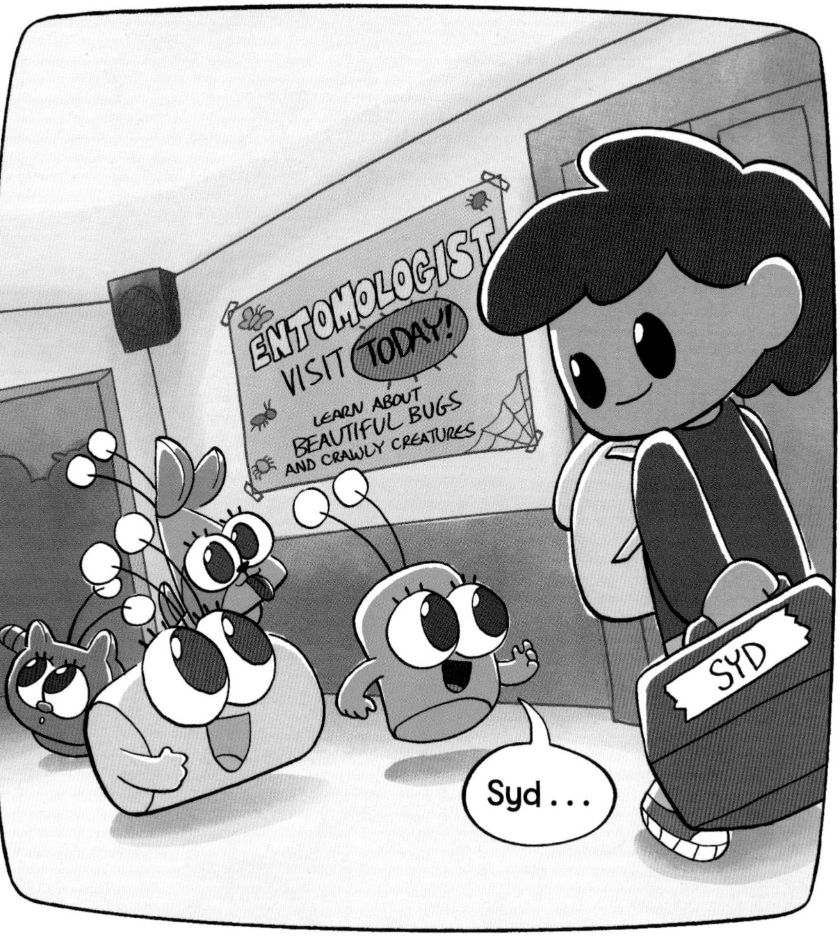
ENTOMOLOGIST
VISIT TODAY!
LEARN ABOUT
BEAUTIFUL BUGS
AND CRAWLY CREATURES
SYD
Syd . . .

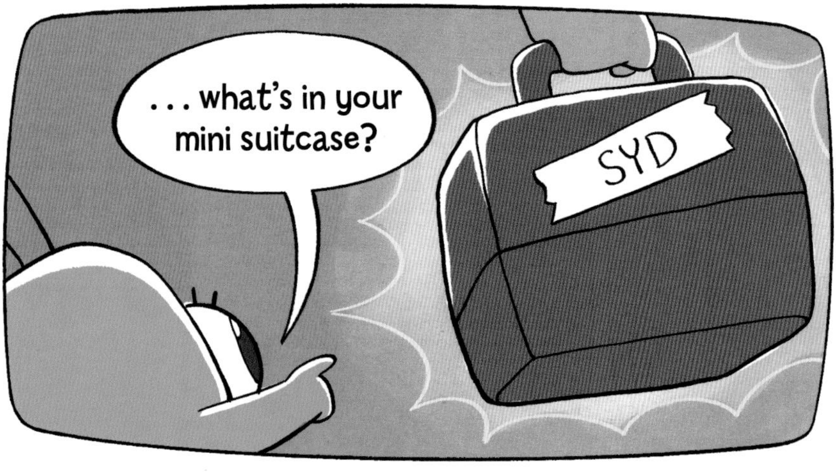
. . . what's in your mini suitcase?
SYD

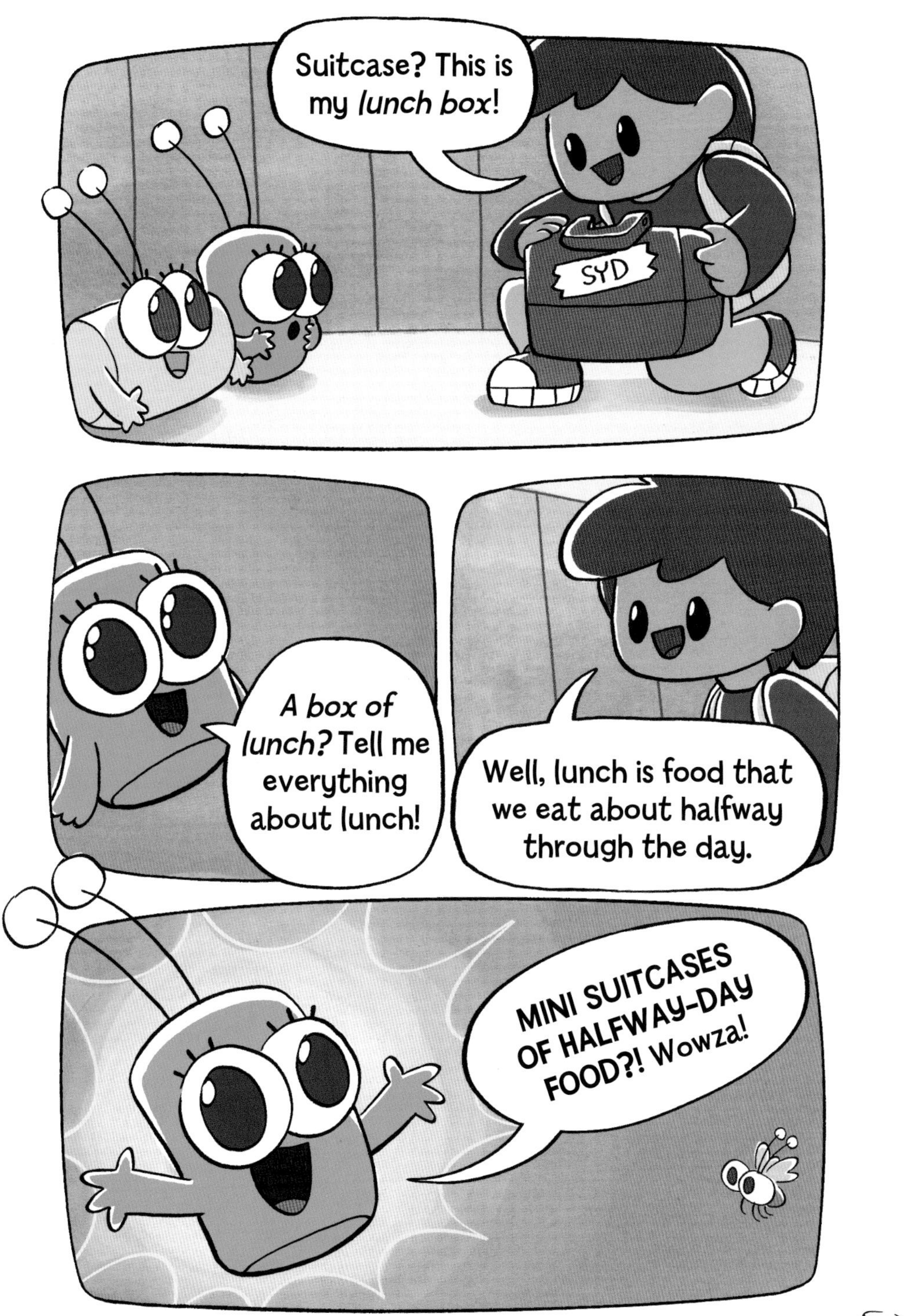
Suitcase? This is my *lunch box*!
SYD
A box of lunch? Tell me everything about lunch!
Well, lunch is food that we eat about halfway through the day.
MINI SUITCASES OF HALFWAY-DAY FOOD?! Wowza!

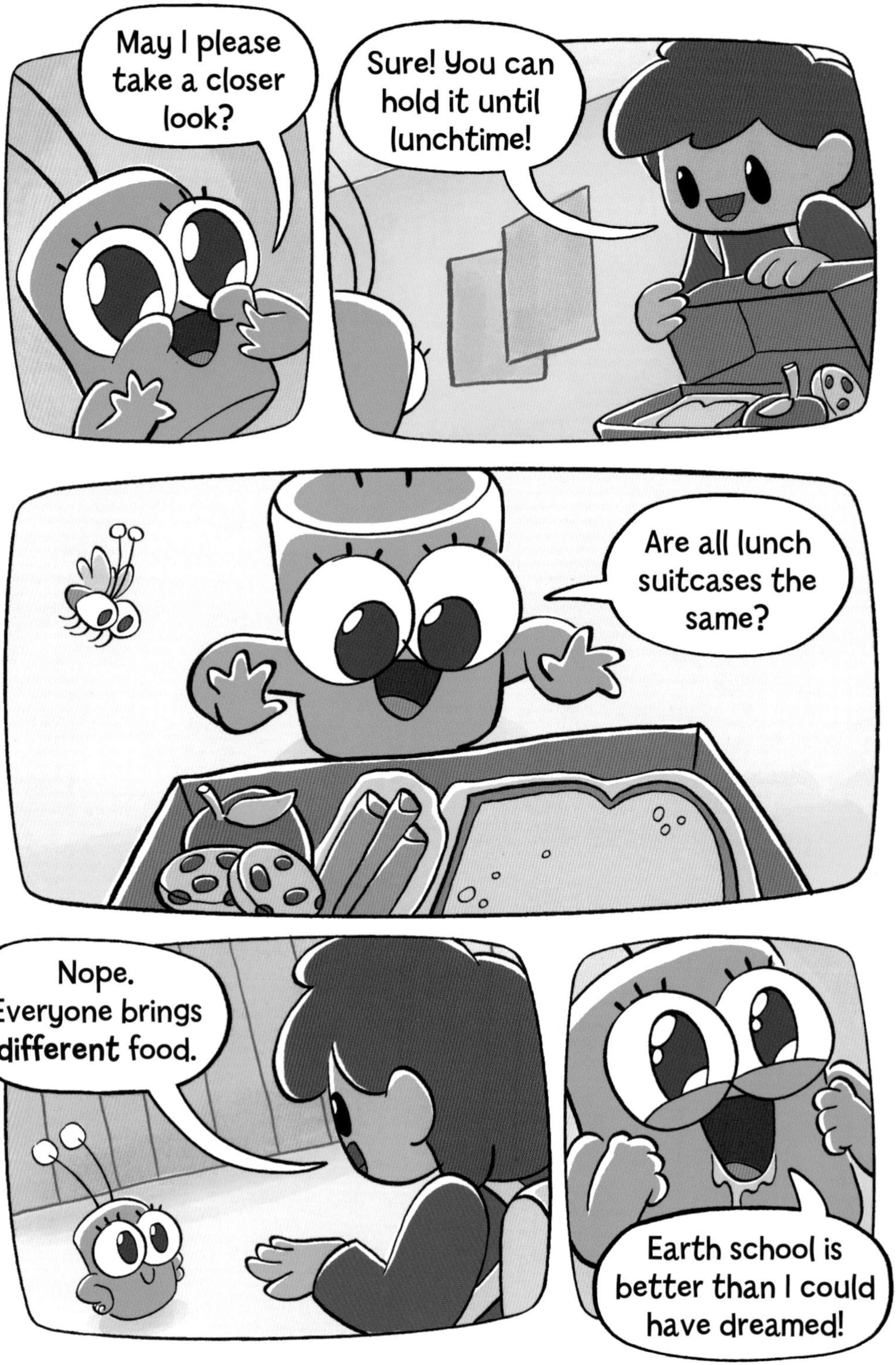
May I please take a closer look?
Sure! You can hold it until lunchtime!
Are all lunch suitcases the same?
Nope. Everyone brings **different** food.
Earth school is better than I could have dreamed!

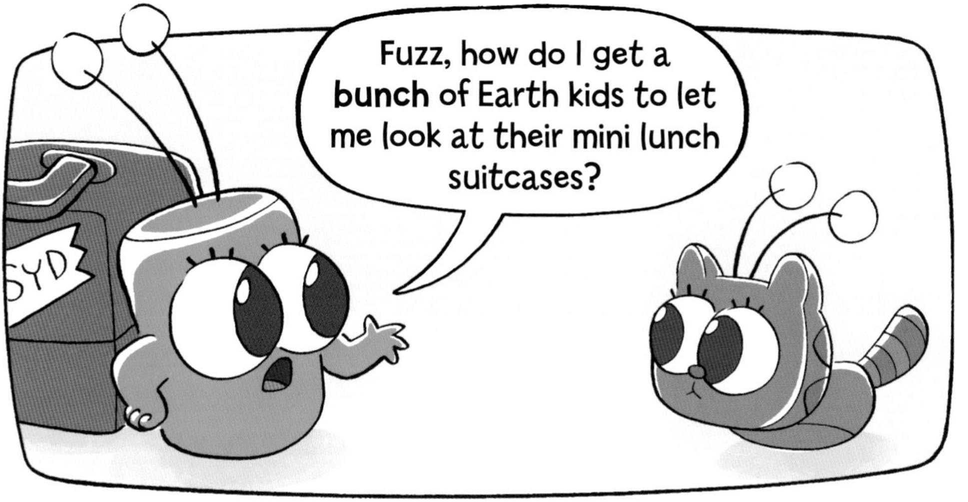

Fuzz, how do I get a **bunch** of Earth kids to let me look at their mini lunch suitcases?
SYD

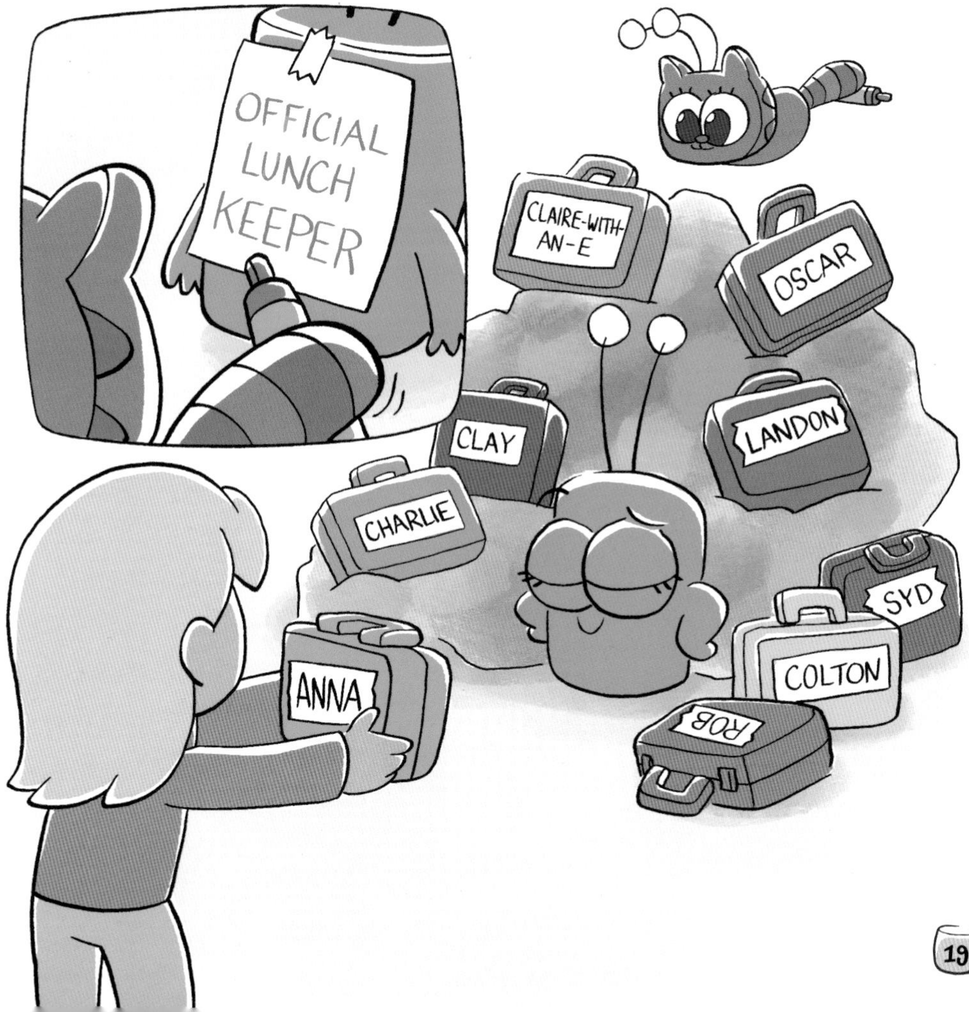

OFFICIAL LUNCH KEEPER
CLAIRE-WITH-AN-E
OSCAR
CLAY
LANDON
CHARLIE
SYD
COLTON
ANNA
ROB

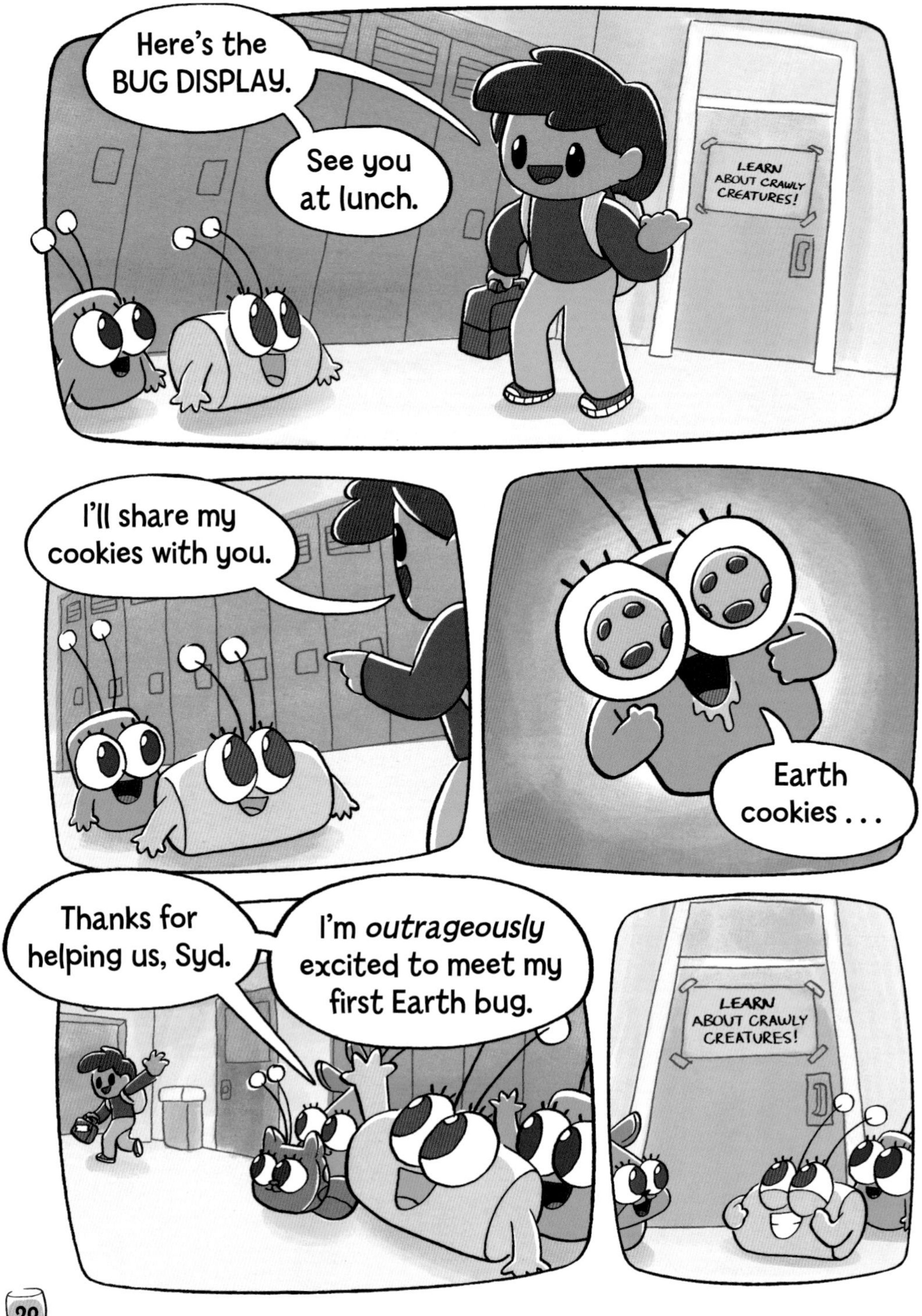
Here's the BUG DISPLAY.
See you at lunch.
LEARN ABOUT CRAWLY CREATURES!
I'll share my cookies with you.
Earth cookies . . .
Thanks for helping us, Syd.
I'm *outrageously* excited to meet my first Earth bug.
LEARN ABOUT CRAWLY CREATURES!

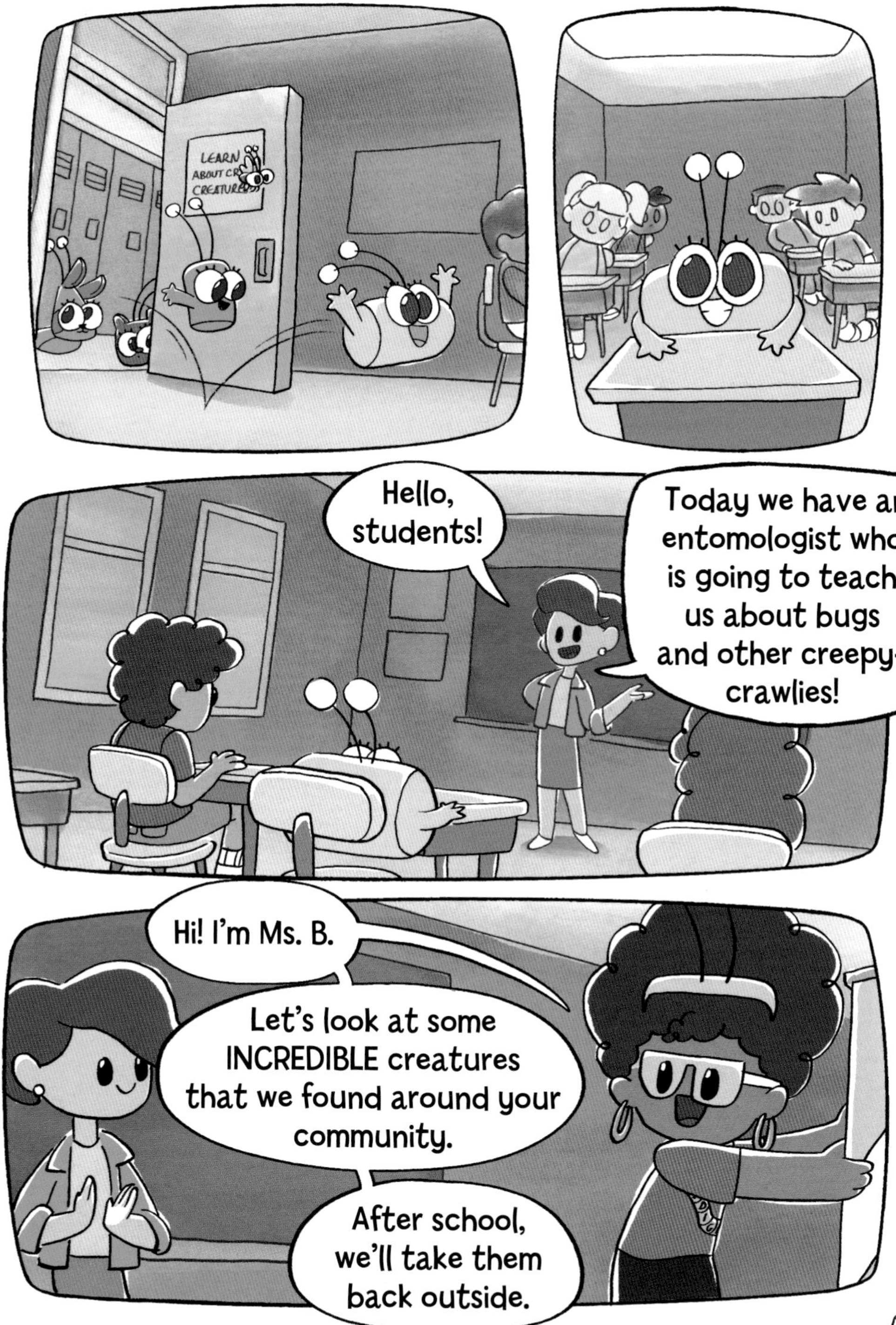
LEARN
ABOUT
Hello, students!
Today we have an entomologist who is going to teach us about bugs and other creepy-crawlies!
Hi! I'm Ms. B.
Let's look at some INCREDIBLE creatures that we found around your community.
After school, we'll take them back outside.

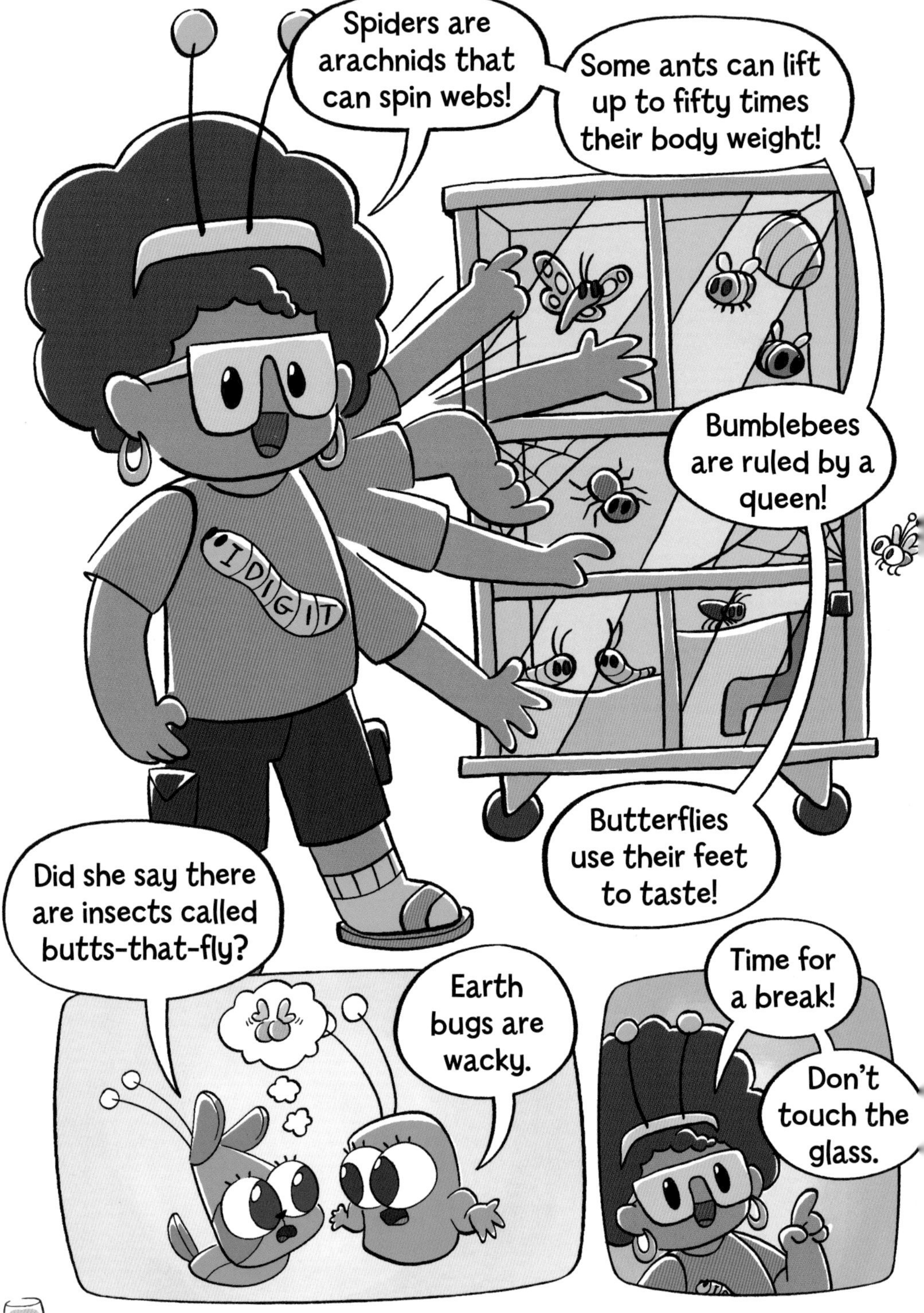
Spiders are arachnids that can spin webs!
Some ants can lift up to fifty times their body weight!
Bumblebees are ruled by a queen!
Butterflies use their feet to taste!
I DIG IT
Did she say there are insects called butts-that-fly?
Earth bugs are wacky.
Time for a break!
Don’t touch the glass.

Chapter 3
Great Escape!

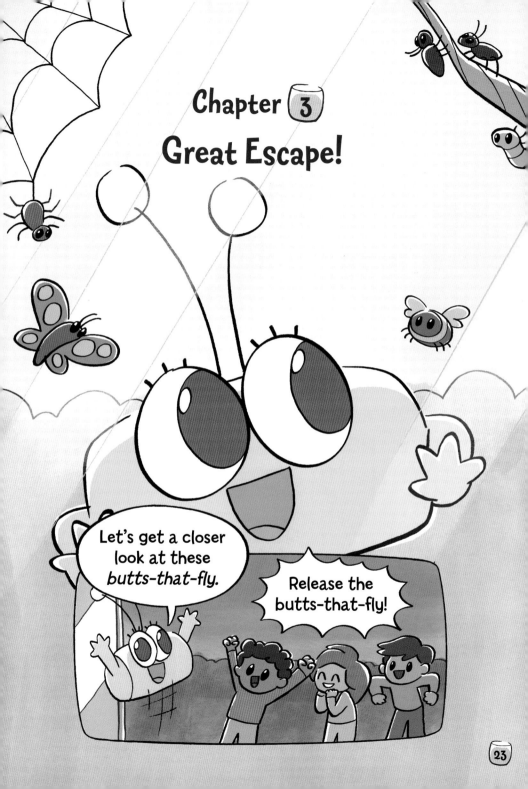

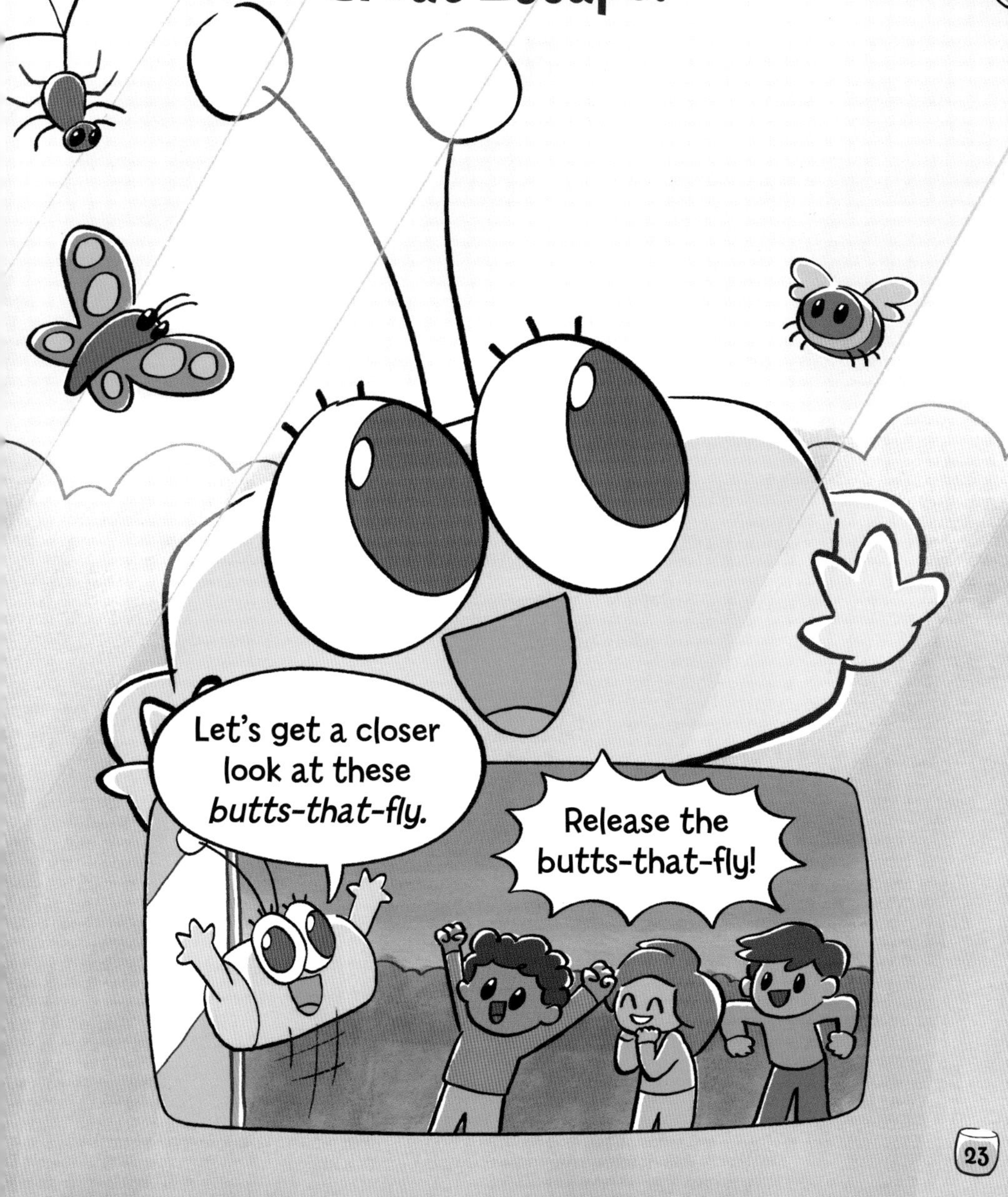
Let's get a closer look at these *butts-that-fly.*
Release the butts-that-fly!

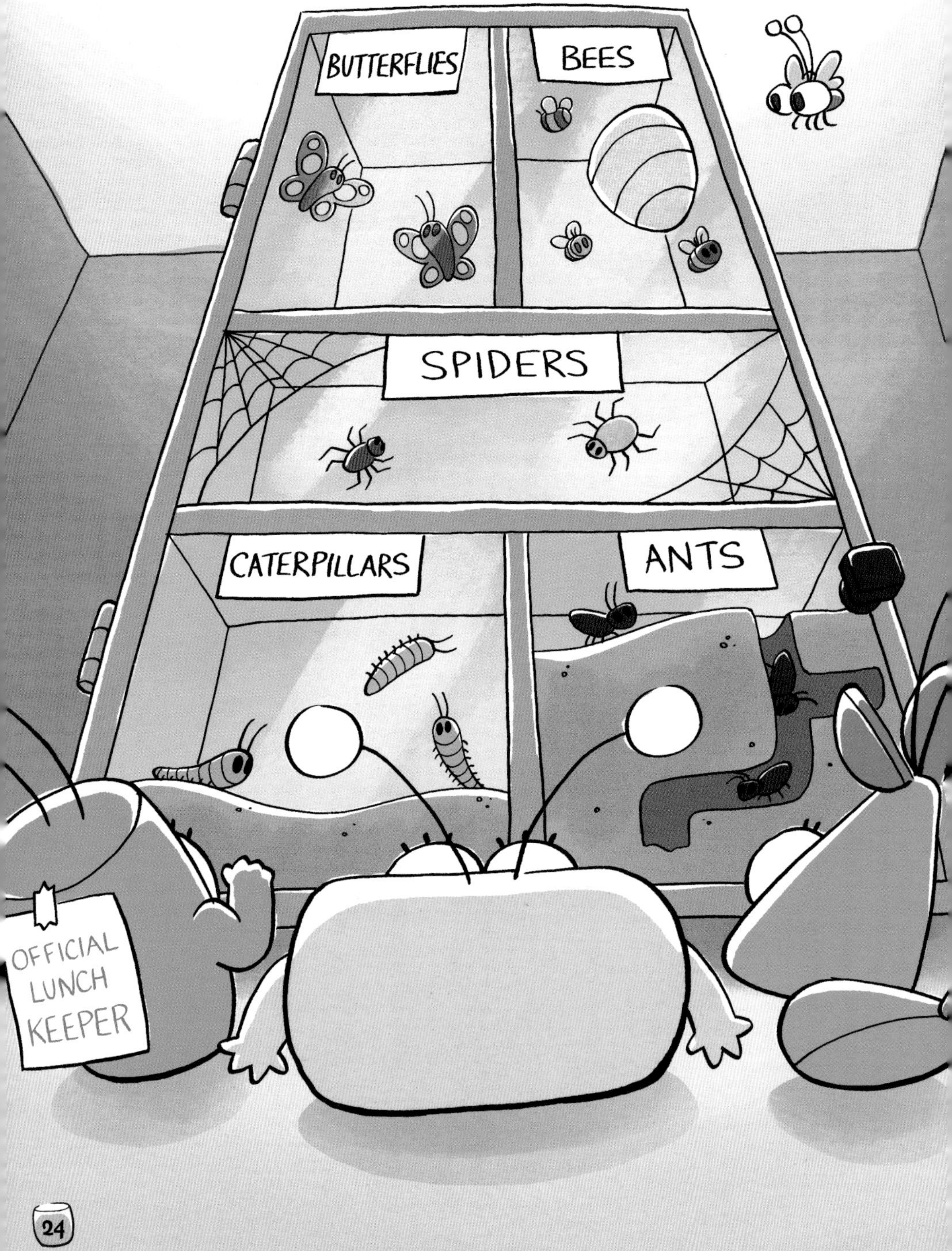
BUTTERFLIES
BEES
SPIDERS
CATERPILLARS
ANTS
OFFICIAL
LUNCH
KEEPER

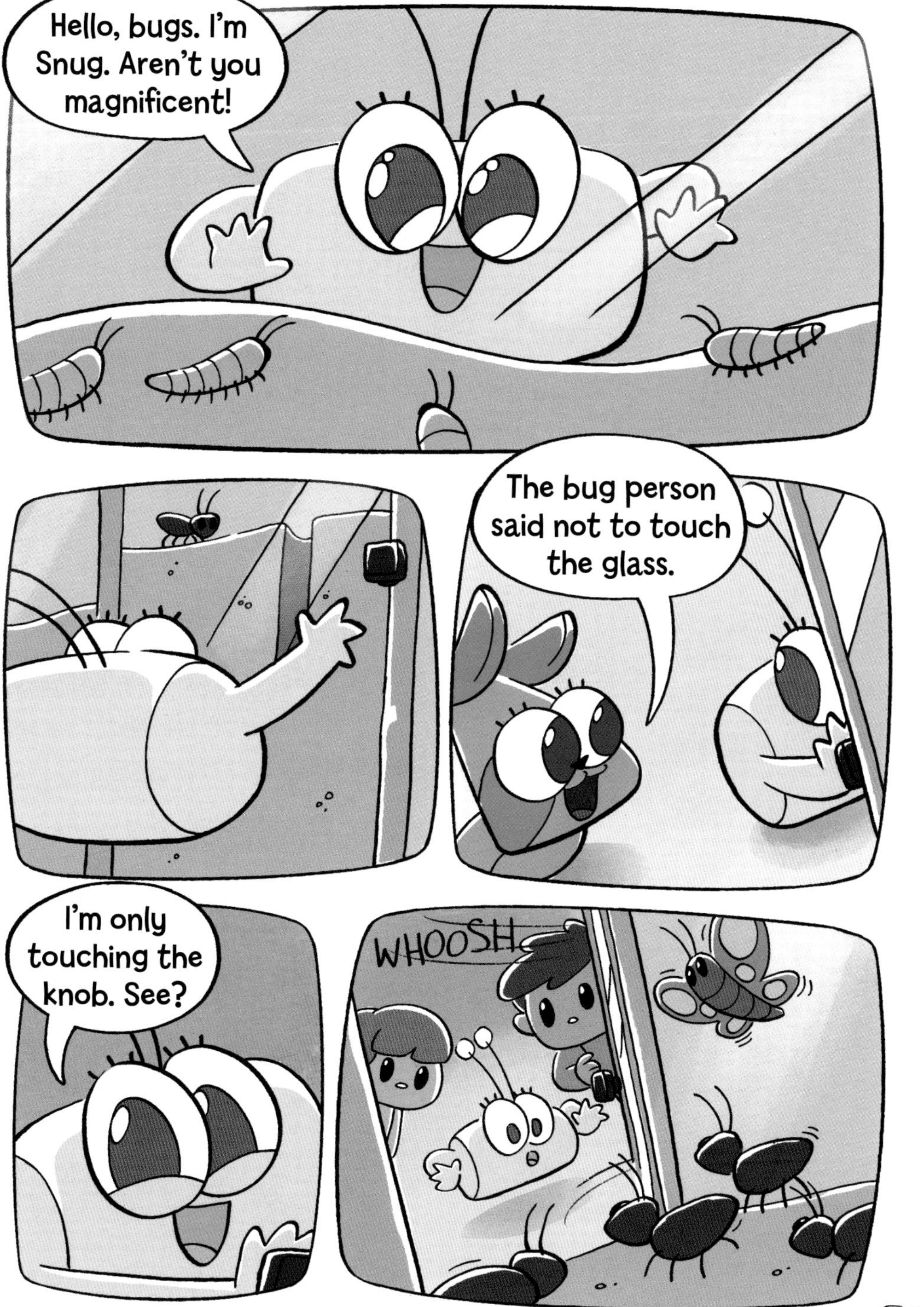
Hello, bugs. I'm Snug. Aren't you magnificent!
The bug person said not to touch the glass.
I'm only touching the knob. See?
WHOOSH

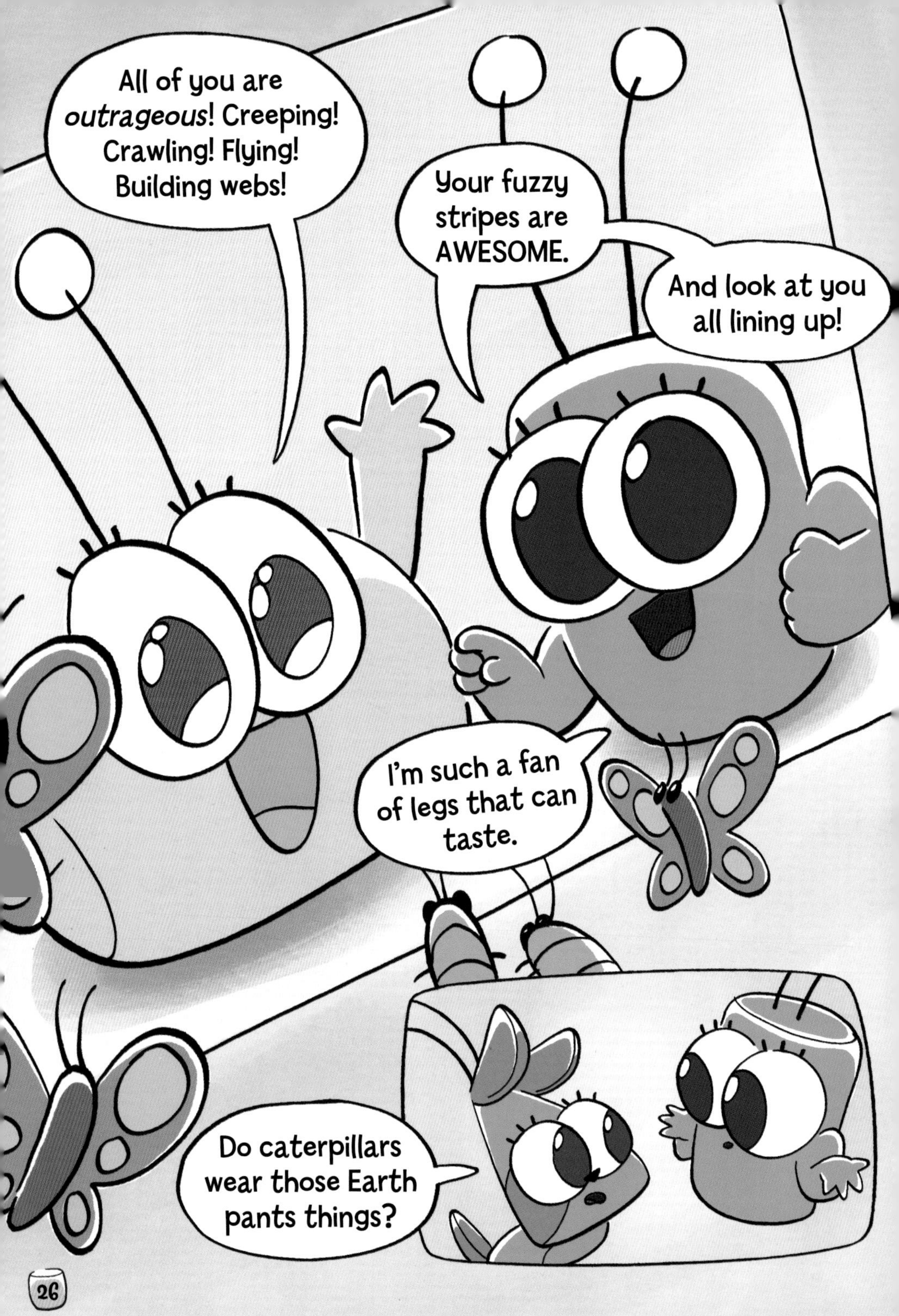
All of you are *outrageous*! Creeping! Crawling! Flying! Building webs!
Your fuzzy stripes are AWESOME.
And look at you all lining up!
I'm such a fan of legs that can taste.
Do caterpillars wear those Earth pants things?

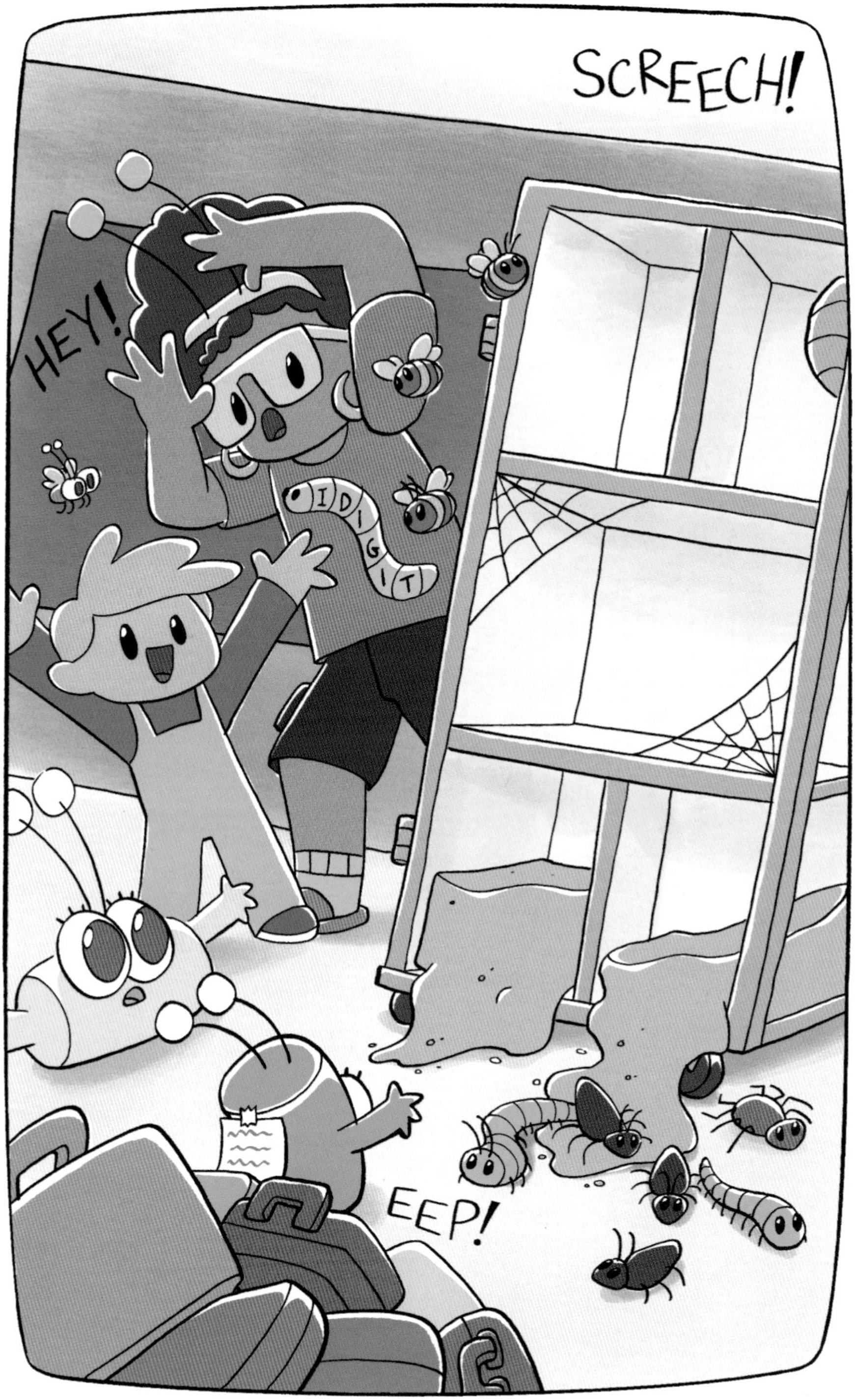
SCREECH!
HEY!
IDIGIT
EEP!

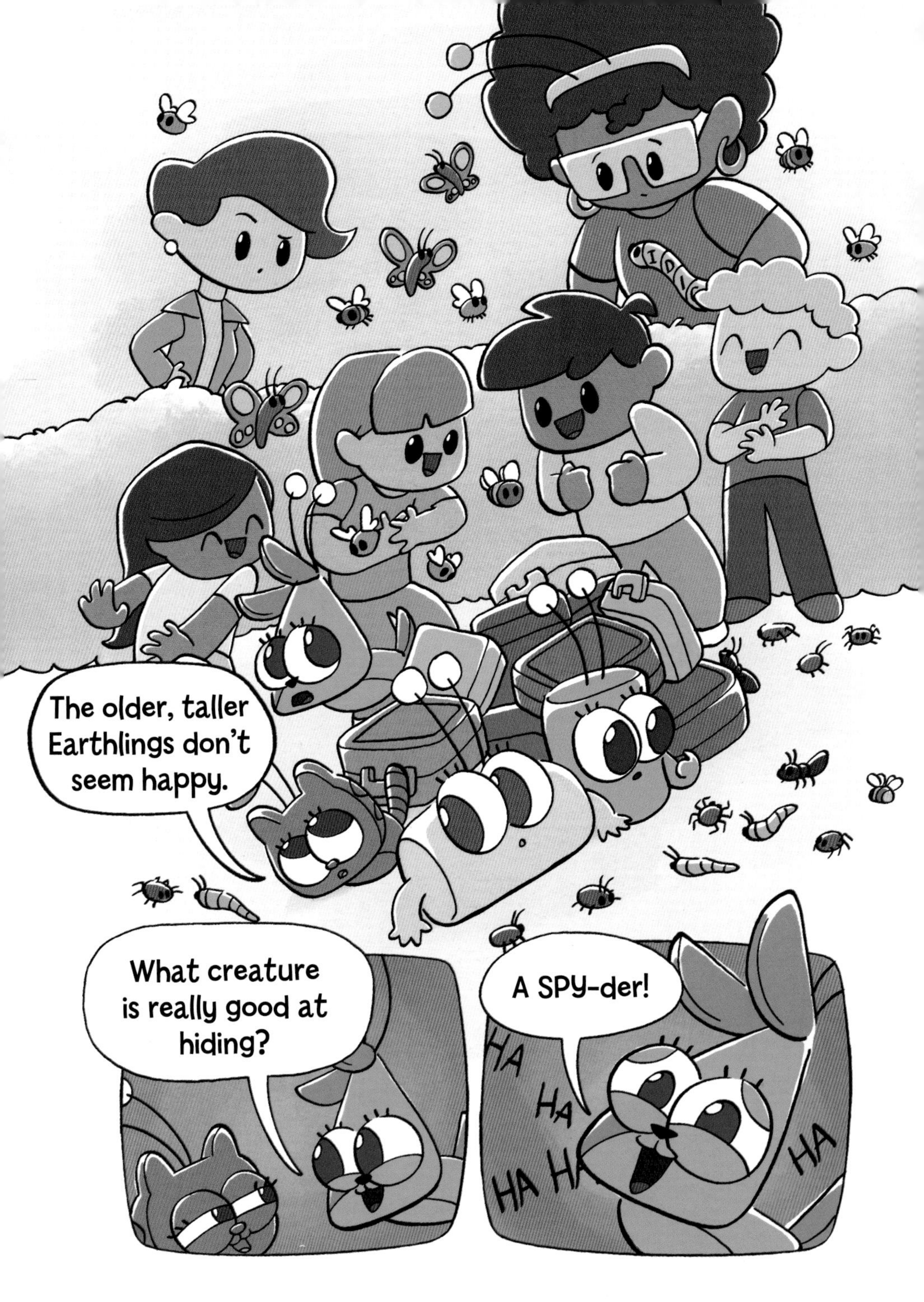
The older, taller Earthlings don't seem happy.
What creature is really good at hiding?
A SPY-der!
HA HA HA HA HA HA

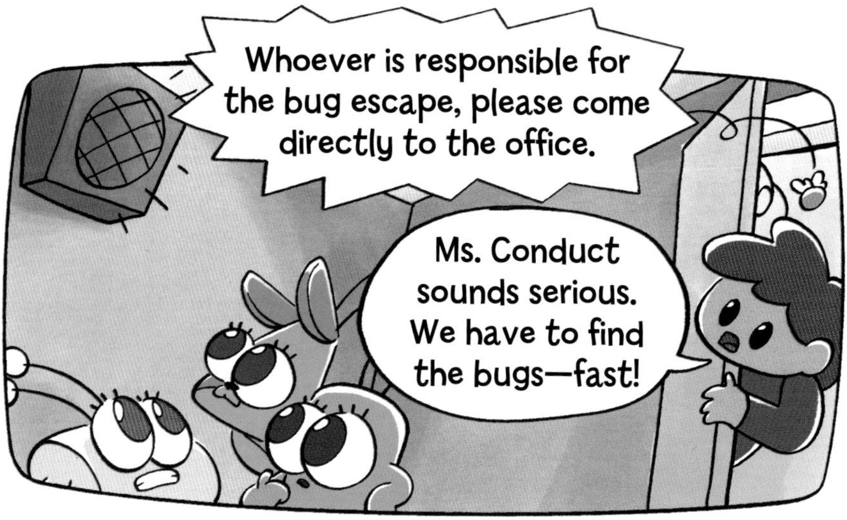
Whoever is responsible for the bug escape, please come directly to the office.
Ms. Conduct sounds serious. We have to find the bugs—fast!

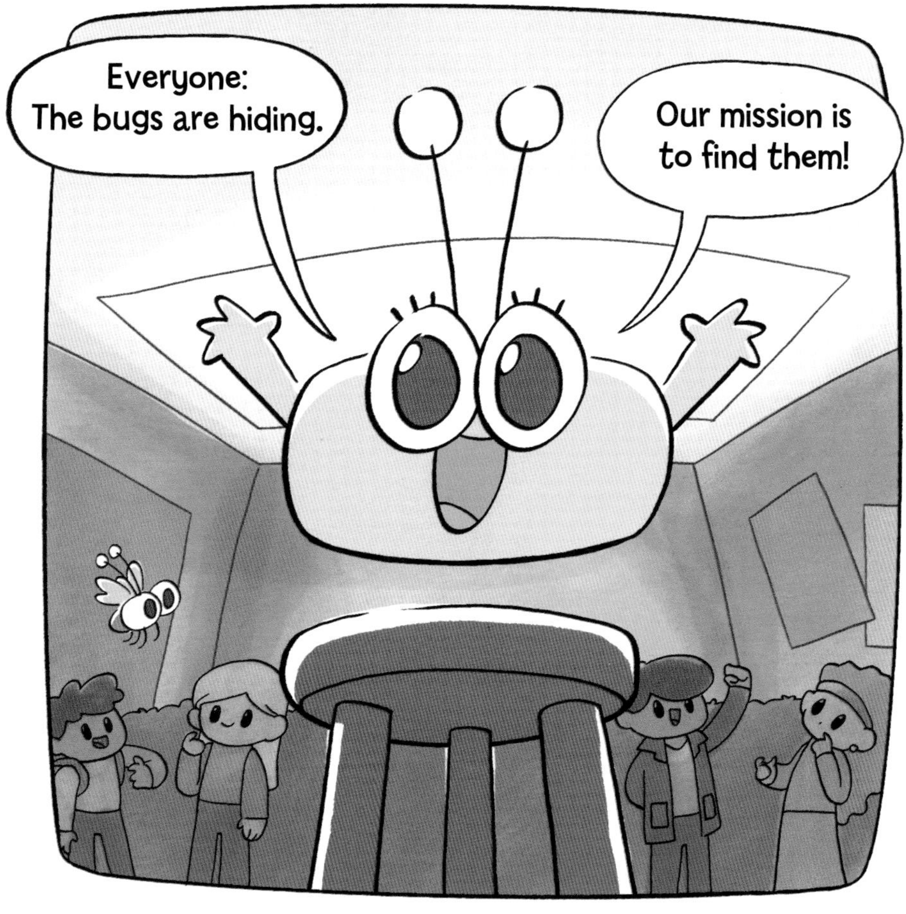
Everyone: The bugs are hiding.
Our mission is to find them!

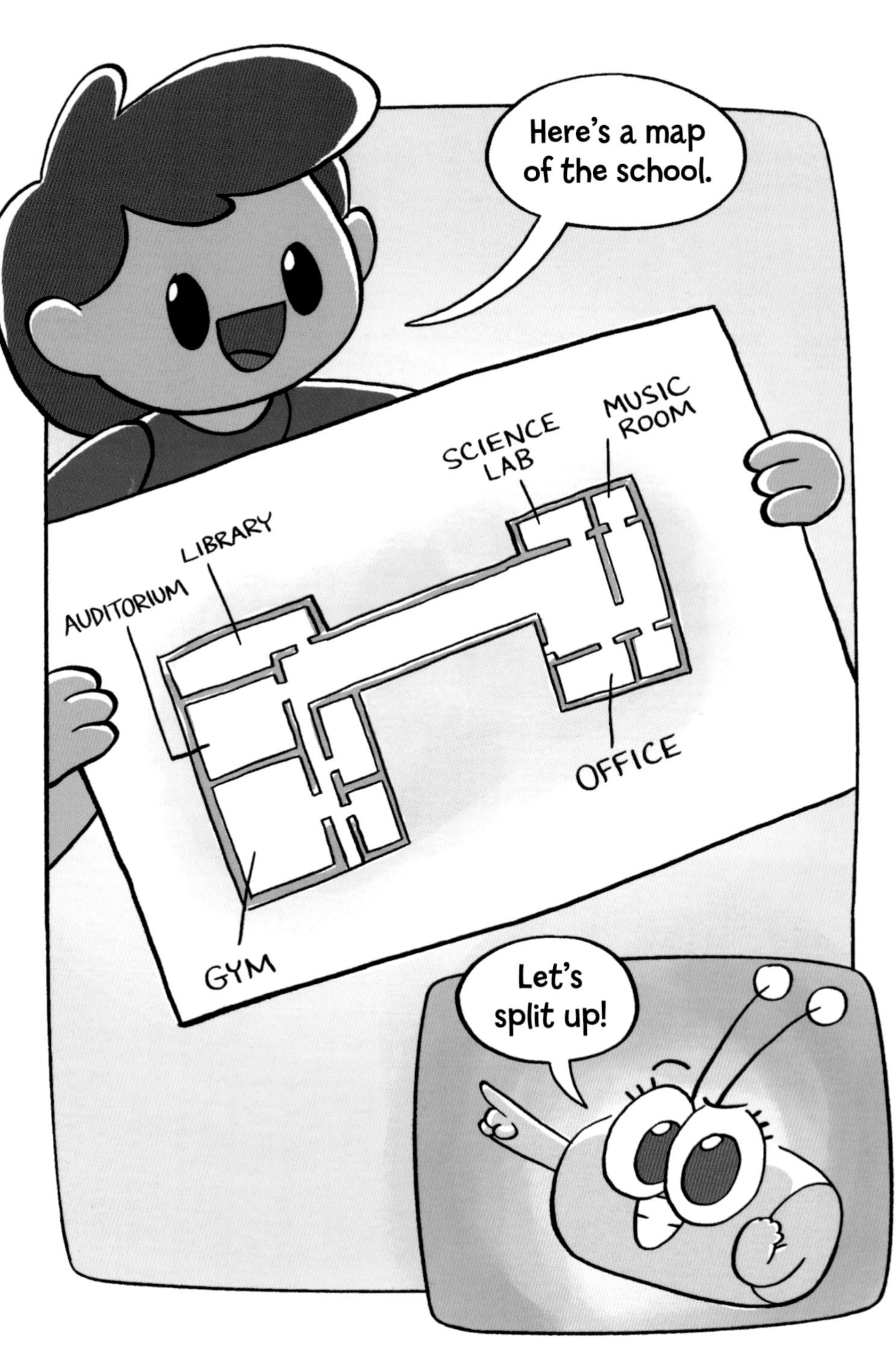
Here's a map of the school.
LIBRARY
AUDITORIUM
SCIENCE LAB
MUSIC ROOM
OFFICE
GYM
Let's split up!

Chapter 4
Bug Hunt!

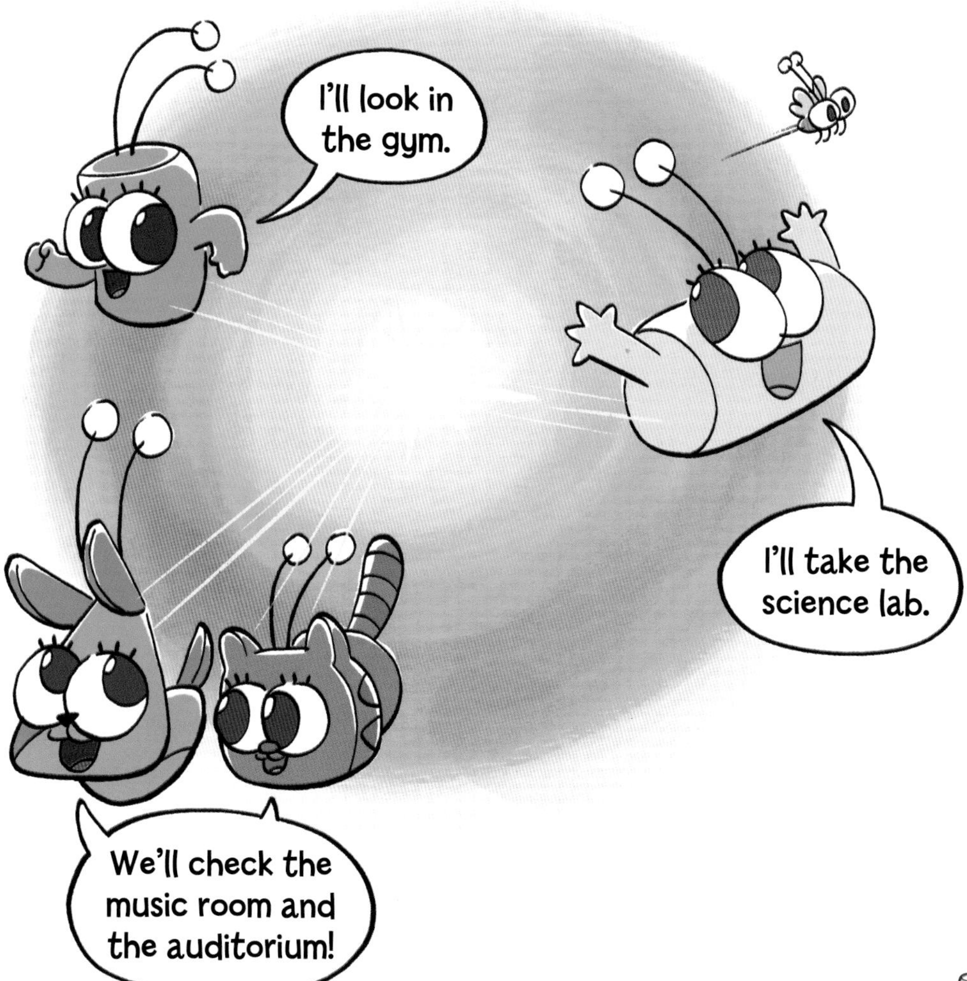
I'll look in the gym.
I'll take the science lab.
We'll check the music room and the auditorium!

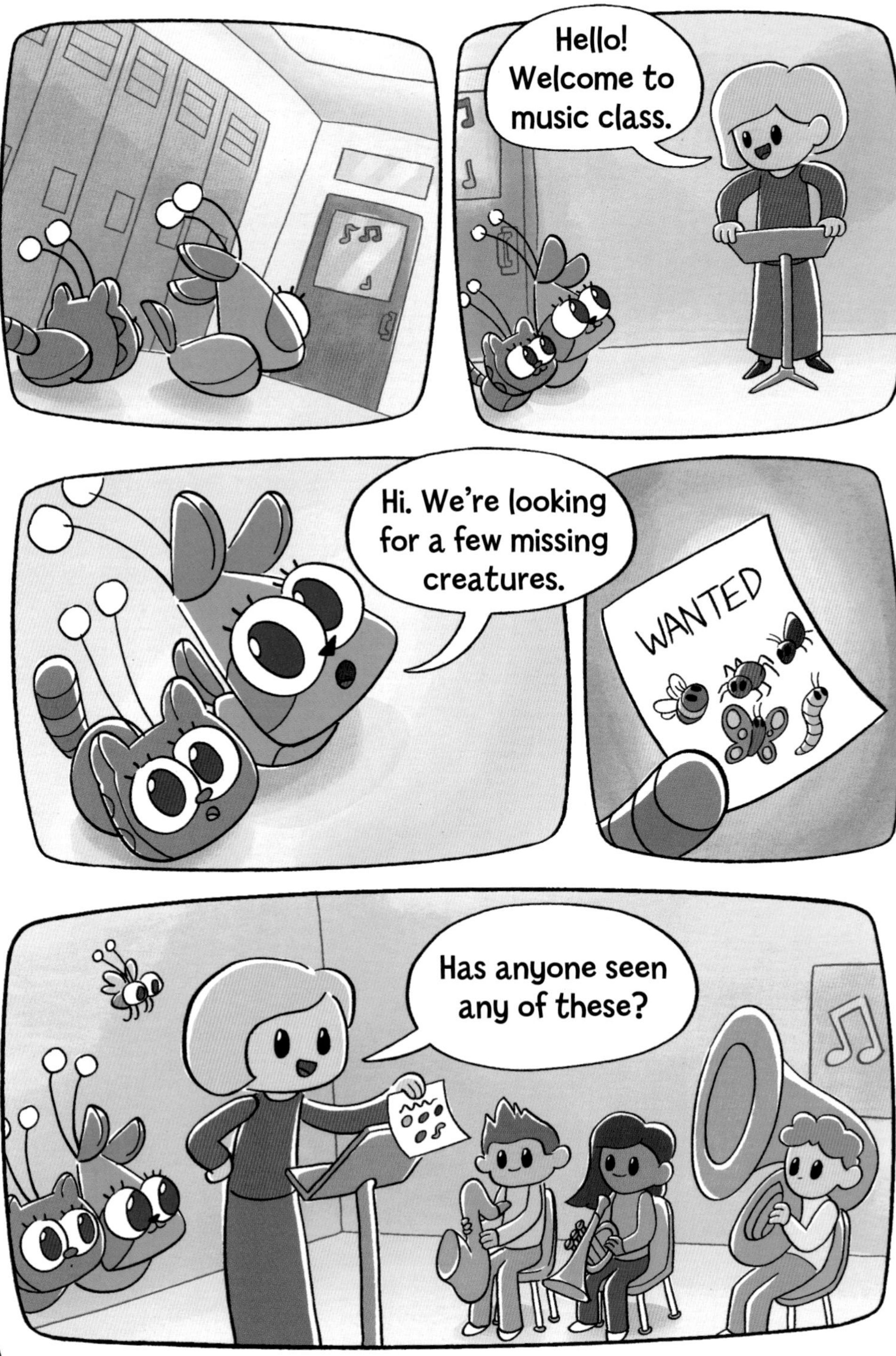
Hello! Welcome to music class.
Hi. We're looking for a few missing creatures.
WANTED
Has anyone seen any of these?

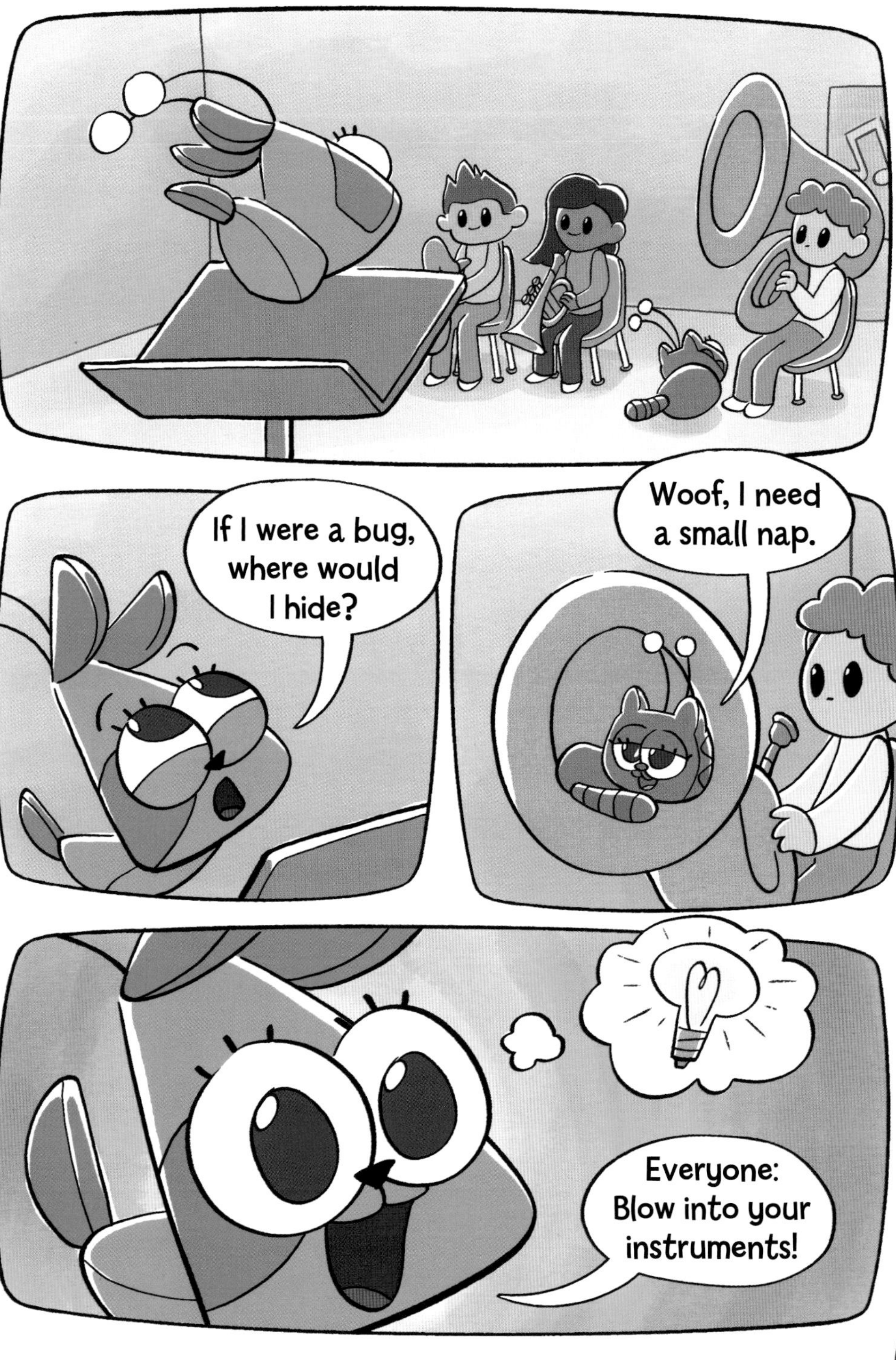
If I were a bug, where would I hide?
Woof, I need a small nap.
Everyone: Blow into your instruments!

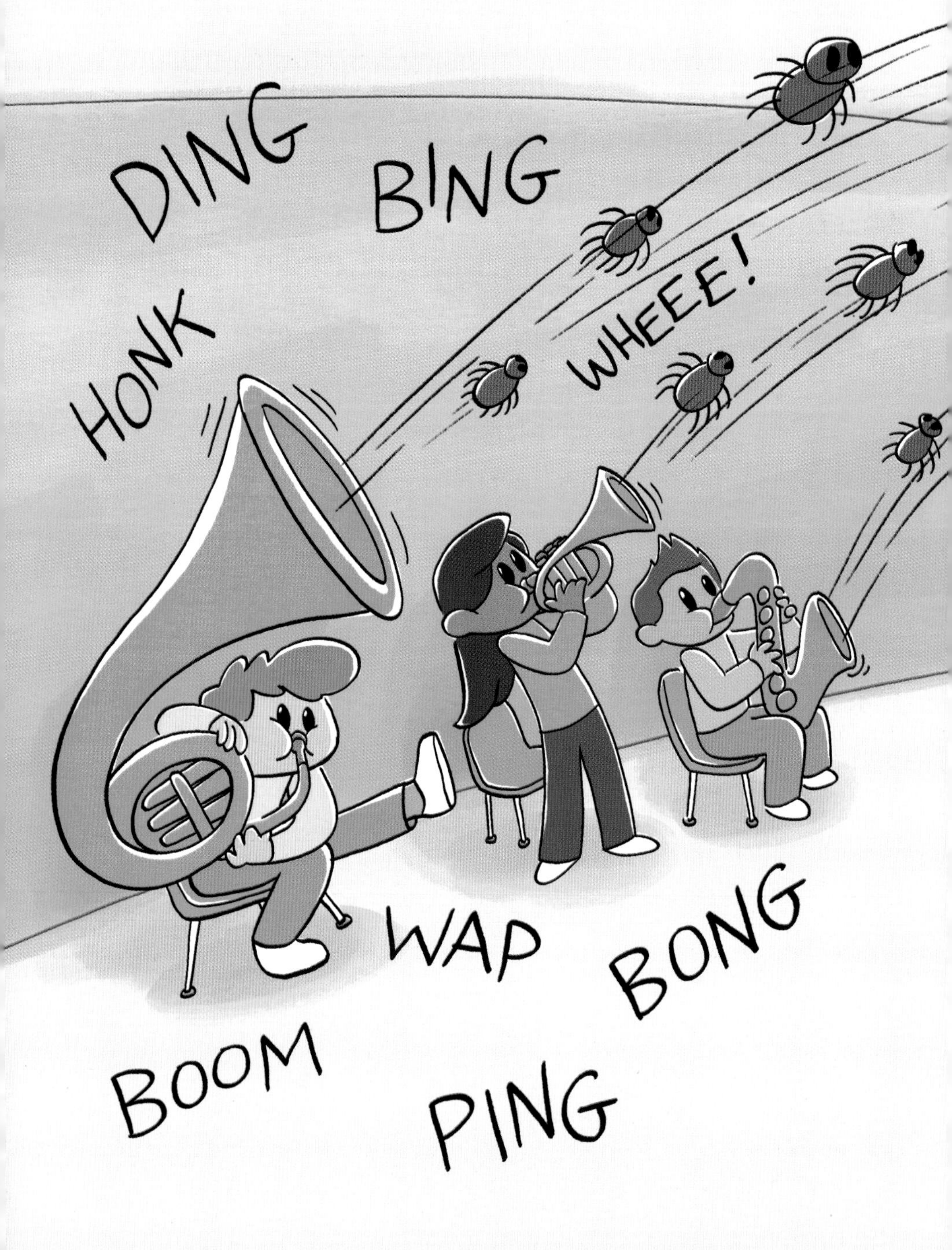
DING
BING
HONK
WHEEE!
WAP
BONG
BOOM
PING

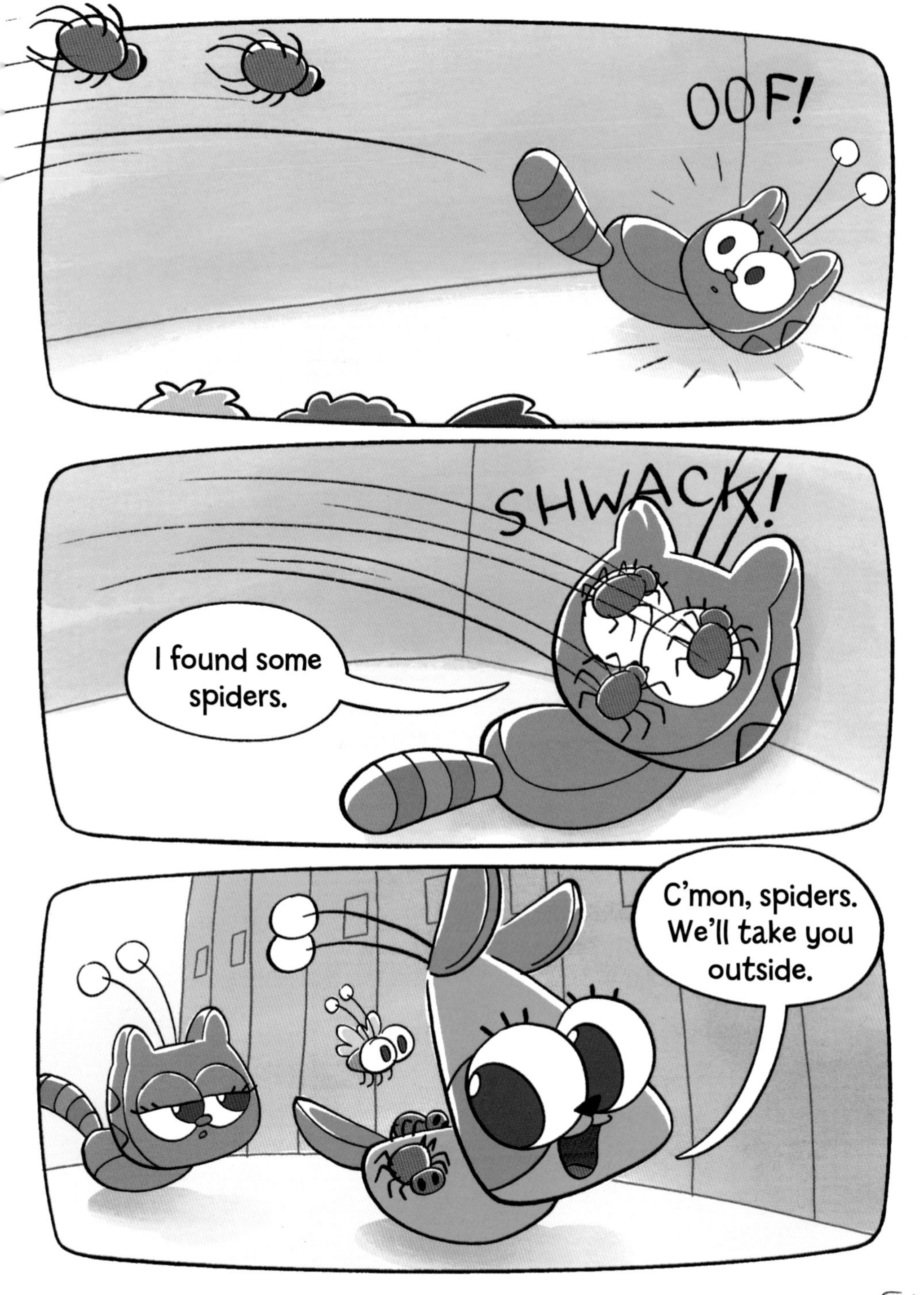
OOF!
SHWACK!
I found some spiders.
C'mon, spiders. We'll take you outside.

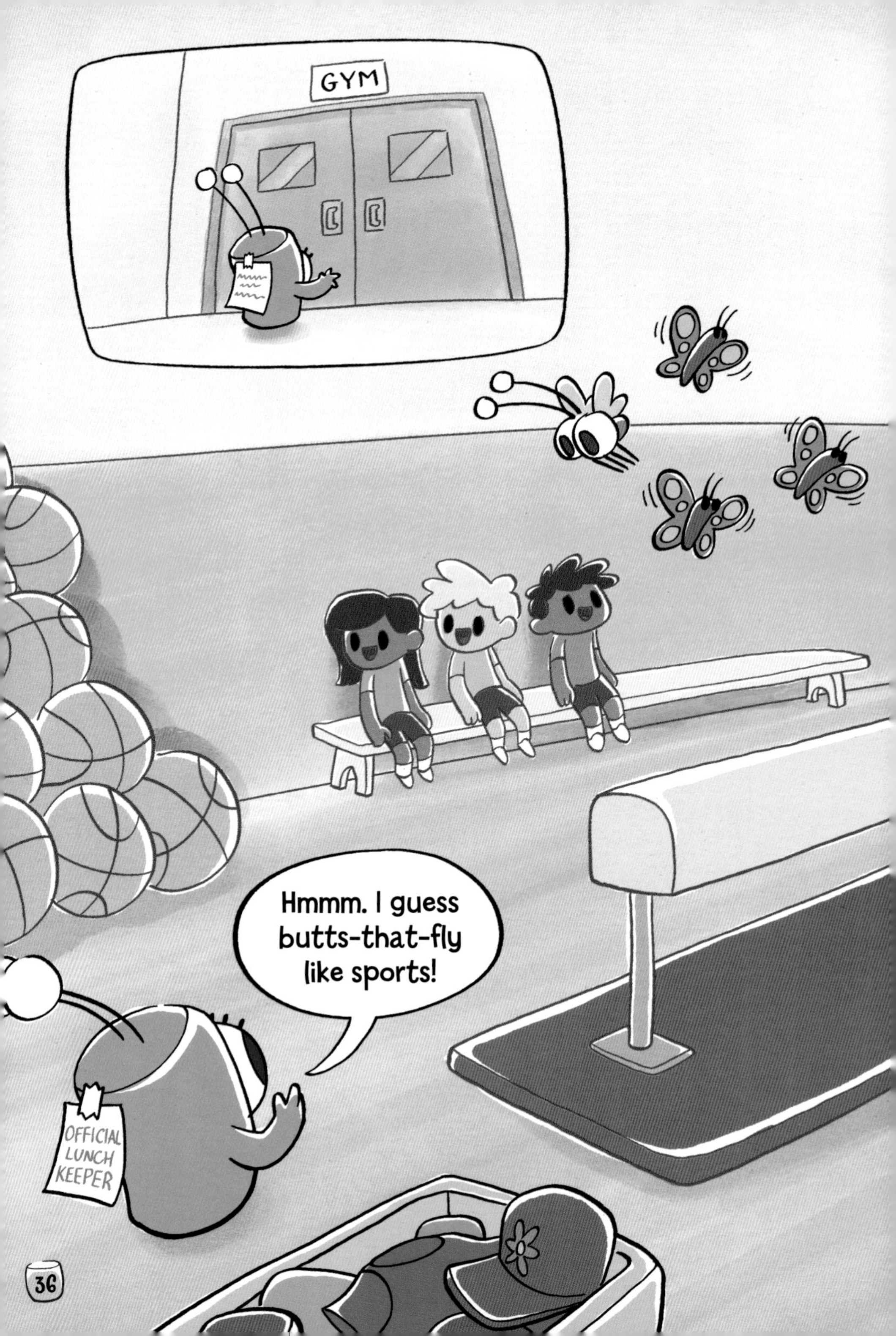
GYM
Hmmm. I guess butts-that-fly like sports!
OFFICIAL LUNCH KEEPER

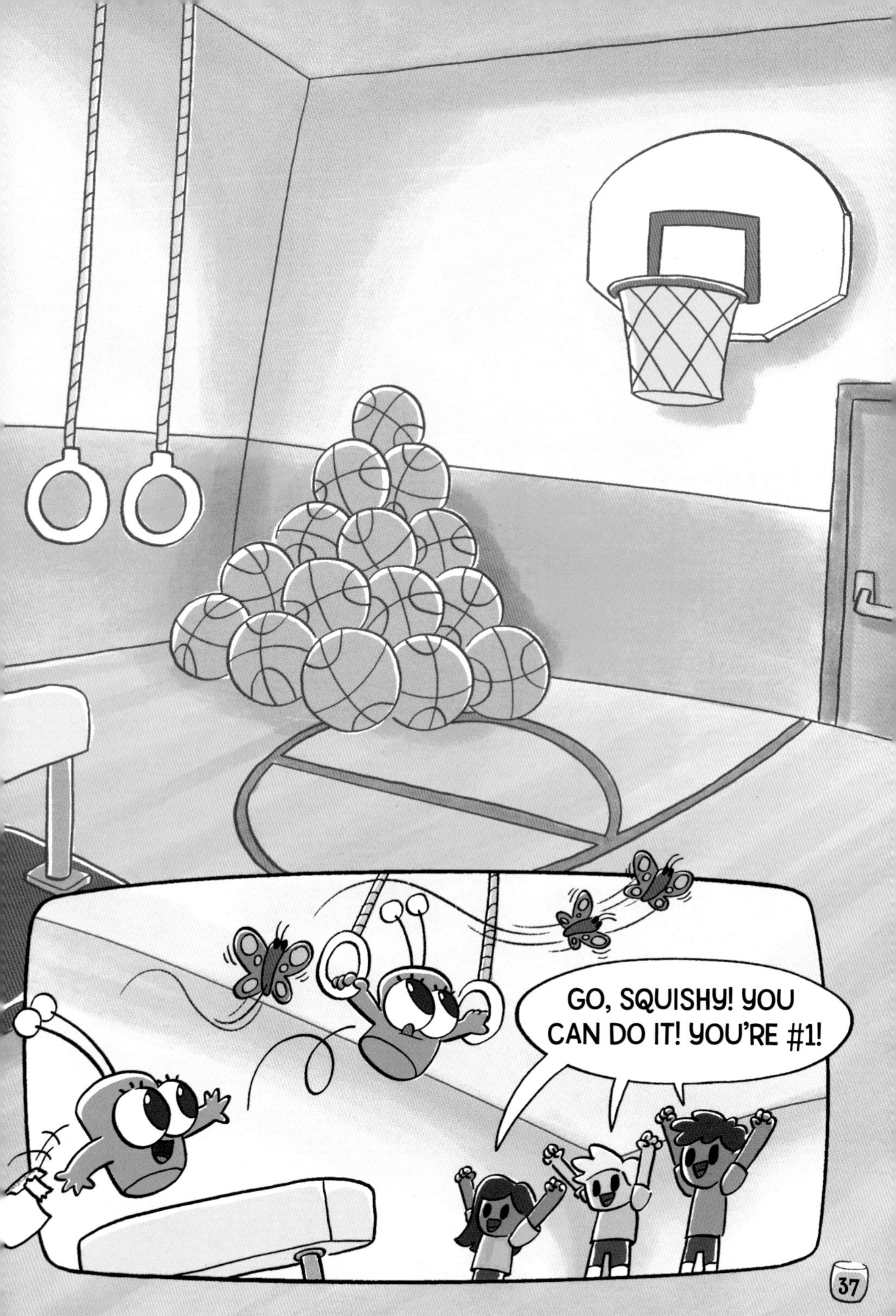
GO, SQUISHY! YOU CAN DO IT! YOU'RE #1!

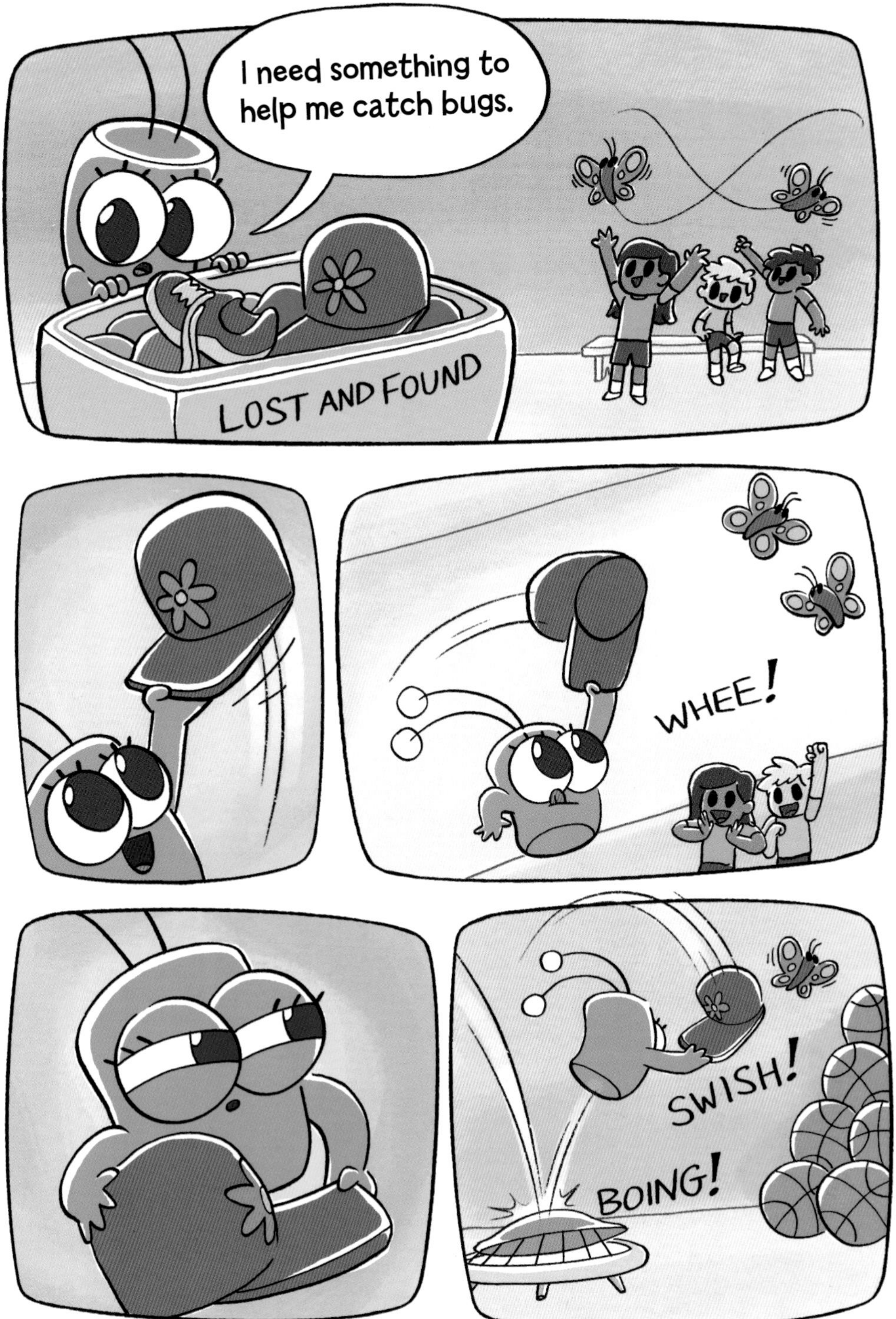
I need something to help me catch bugs.
LOST AND FOUND
WHEE!
SWISH!
BOING!

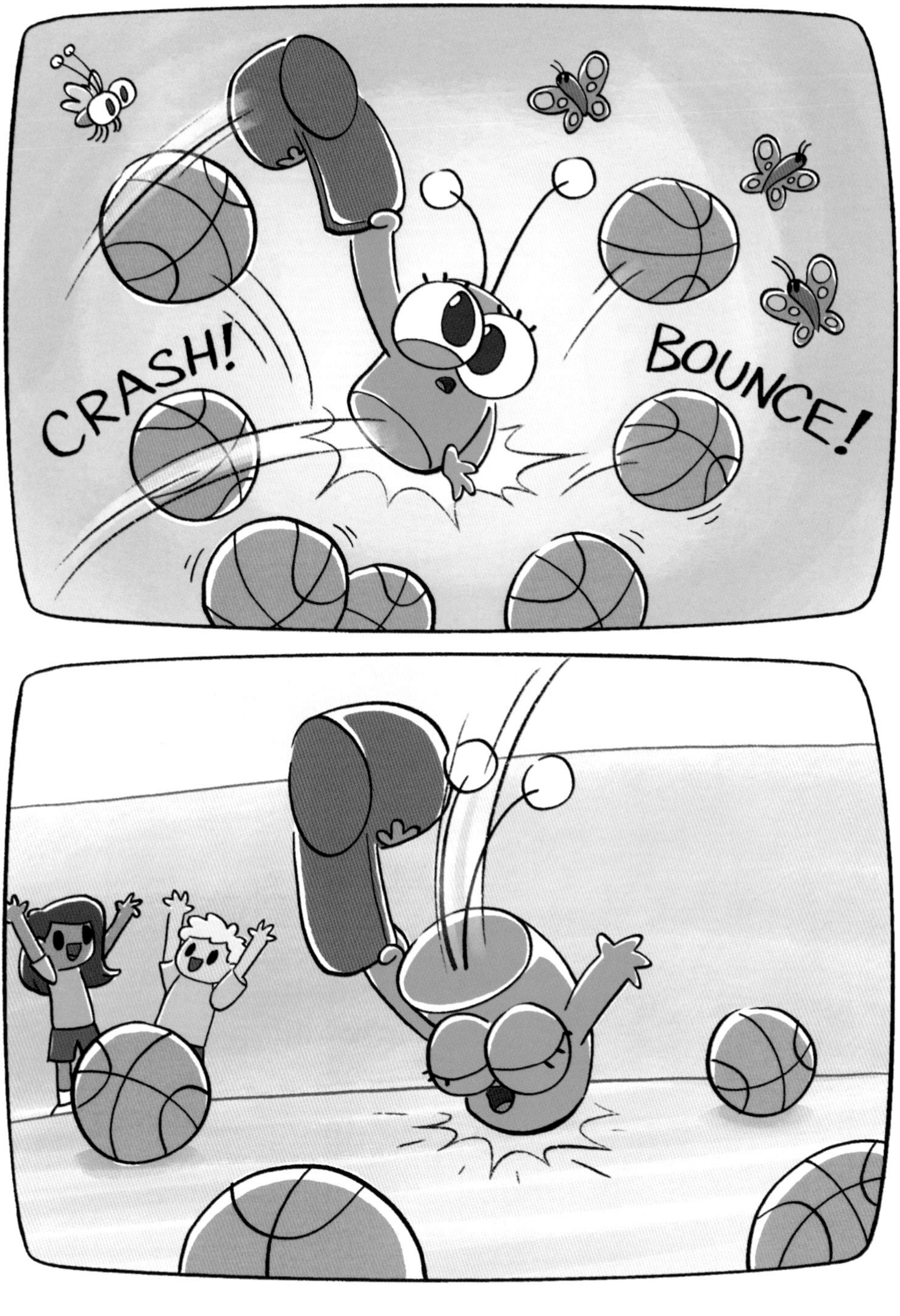
CRASH!
BOUNCE!

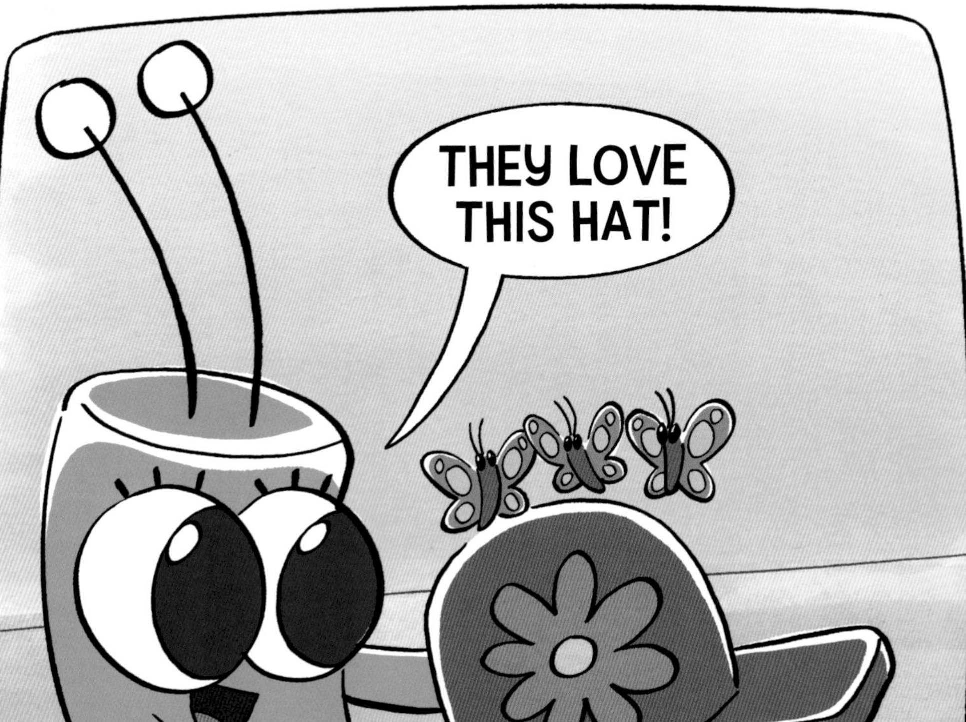
THEY LOVE THIS HAT!

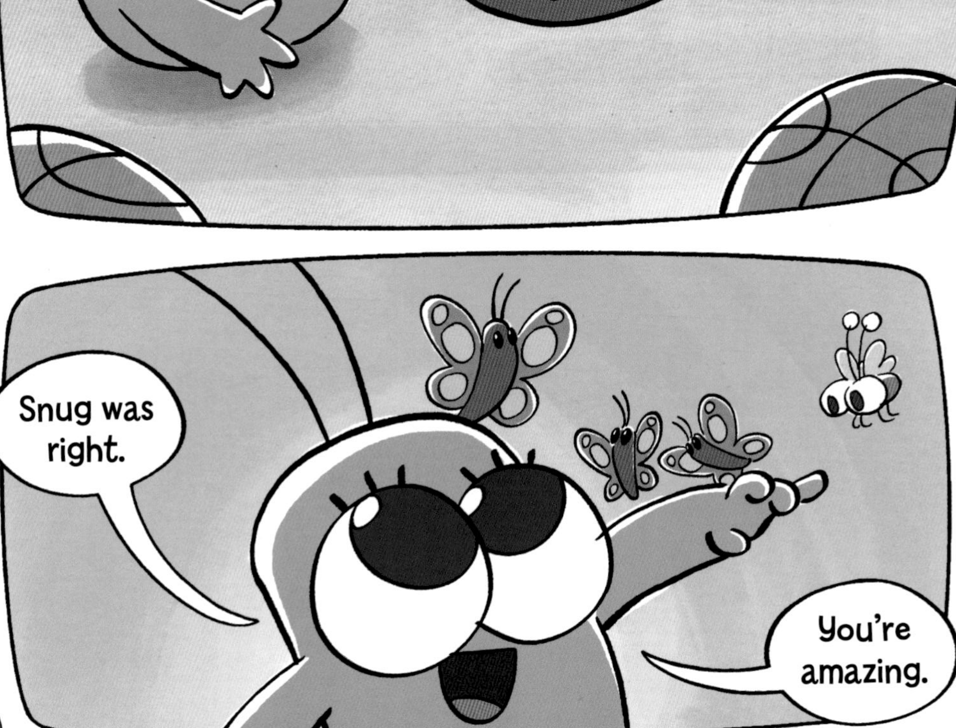
Snug was right.
You're amazing.

Chapter 5

Snug as a Bug in a ~~Rug~~ Volcano?

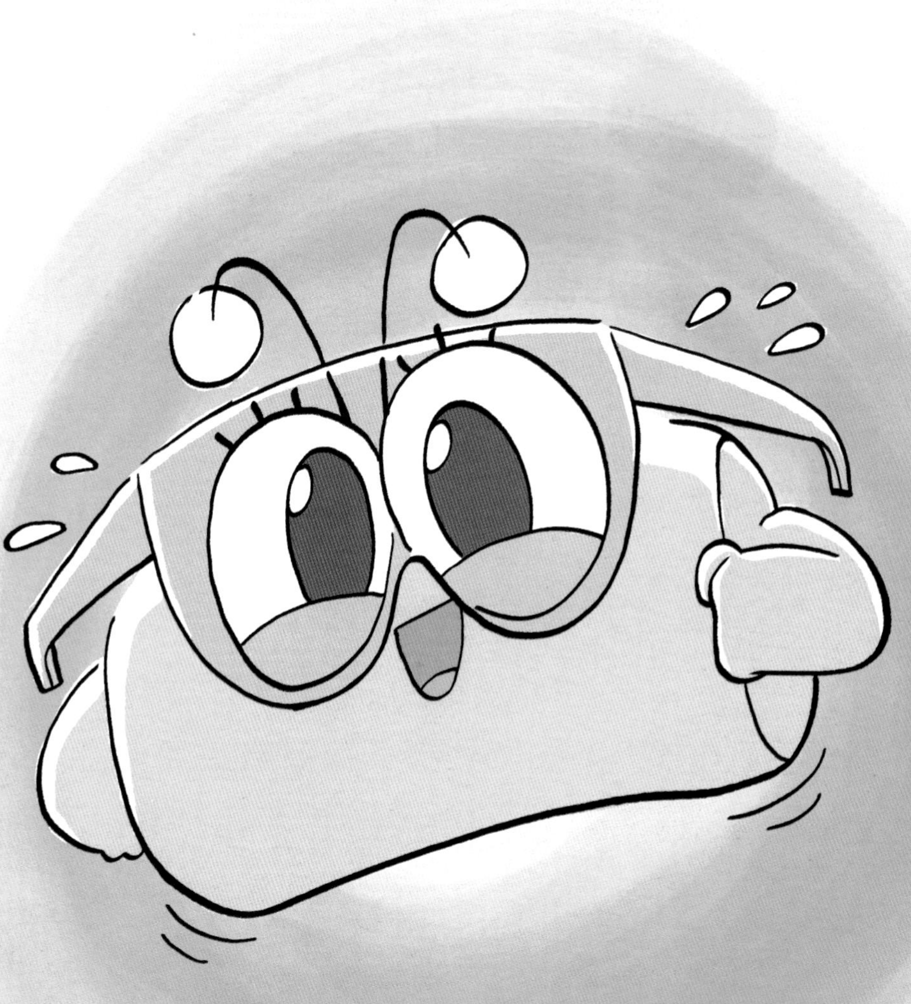

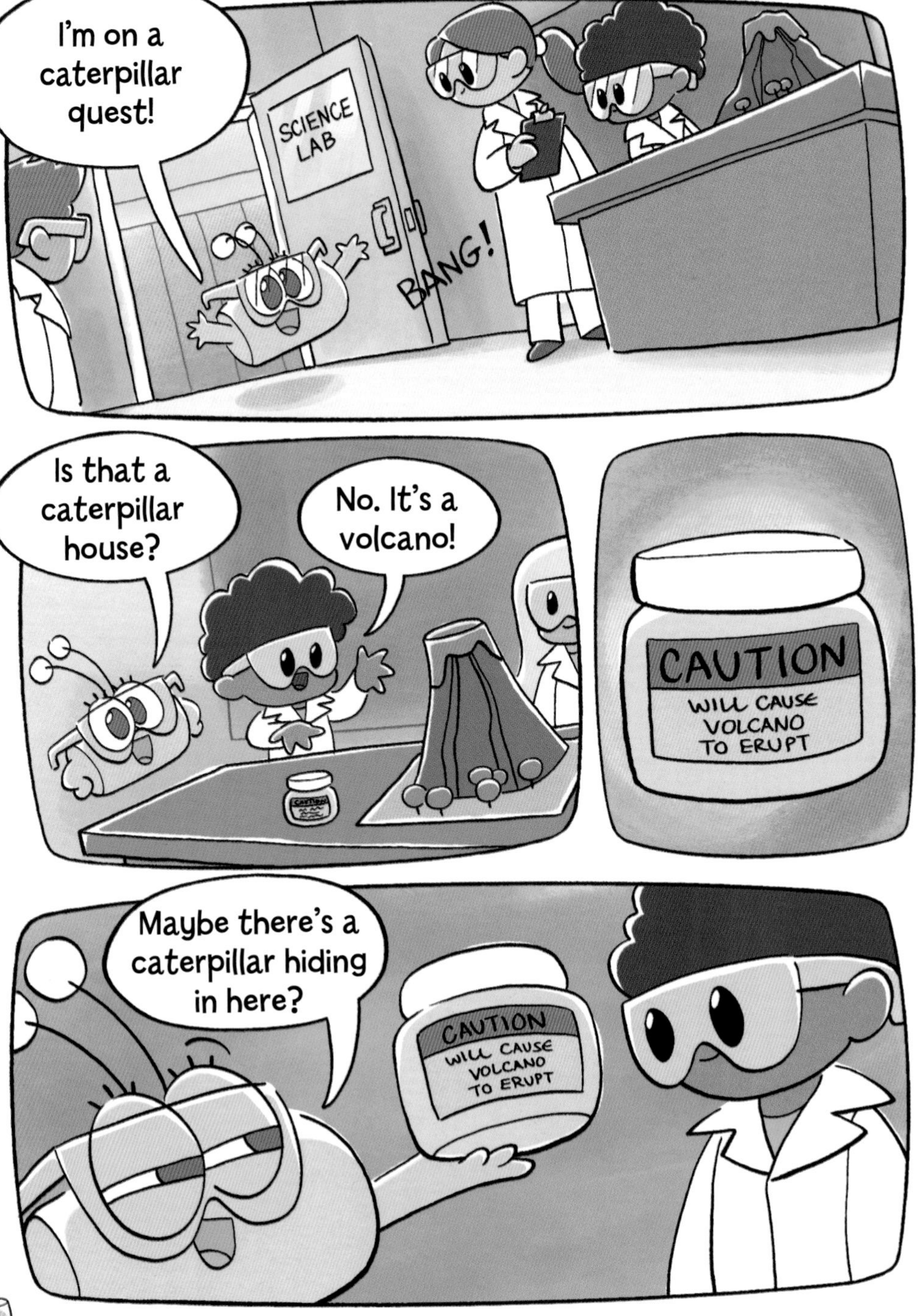
I'm on a caterpillar quest!
SCIENCE LAB
BANG!
Is that a caterpillar house?
No. It's a volcano!
CAUTION
CAUTION
WILL CAUSE VOLCANO TO ERUPT
Maybe there's a caterpillar hiding in here?
CAUTION
WILL CAUSE VOLCANO TO ERUPT

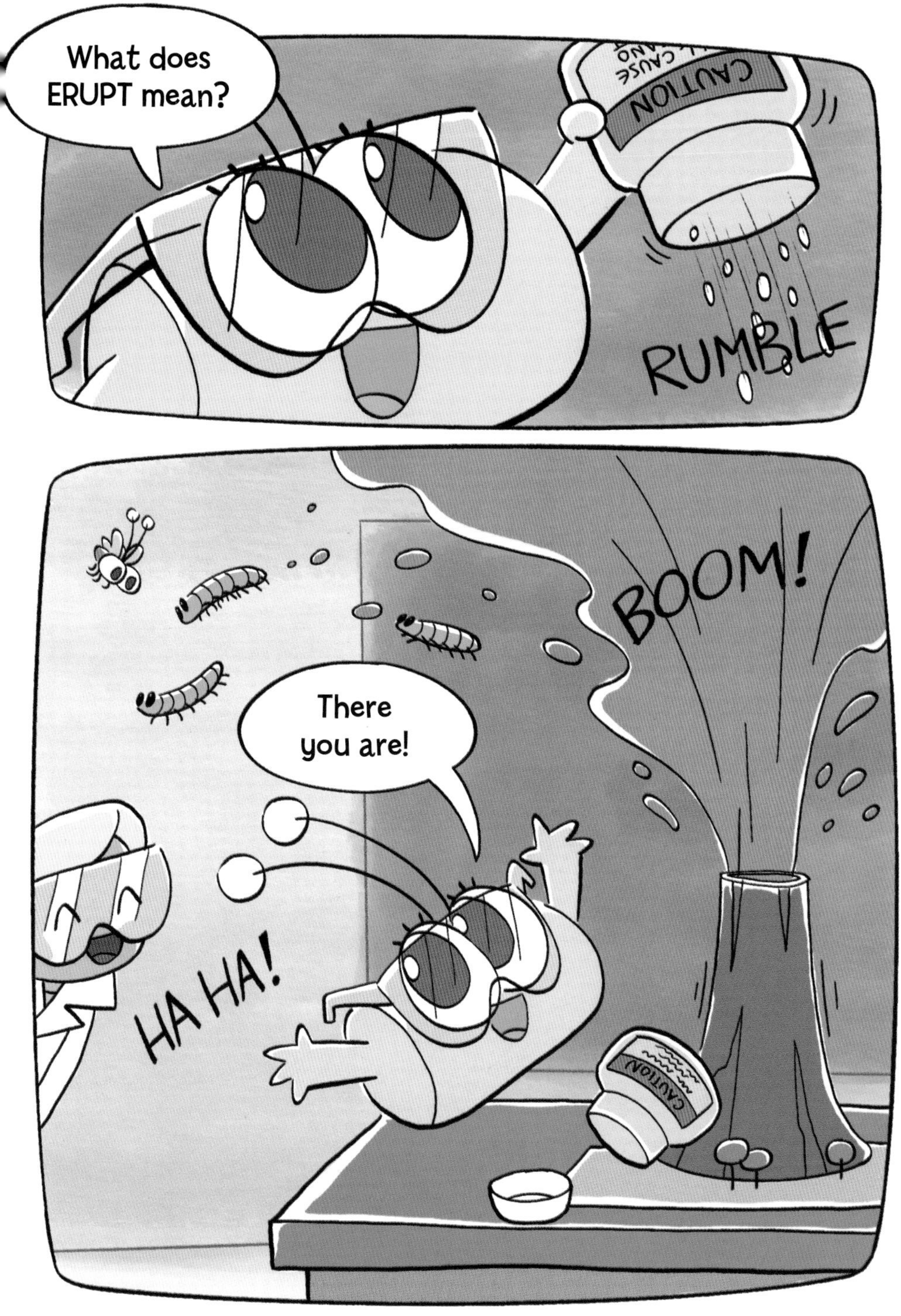
What does ERUPT mean?
RUMBLE
BOOM!
There you are!
HA HA!

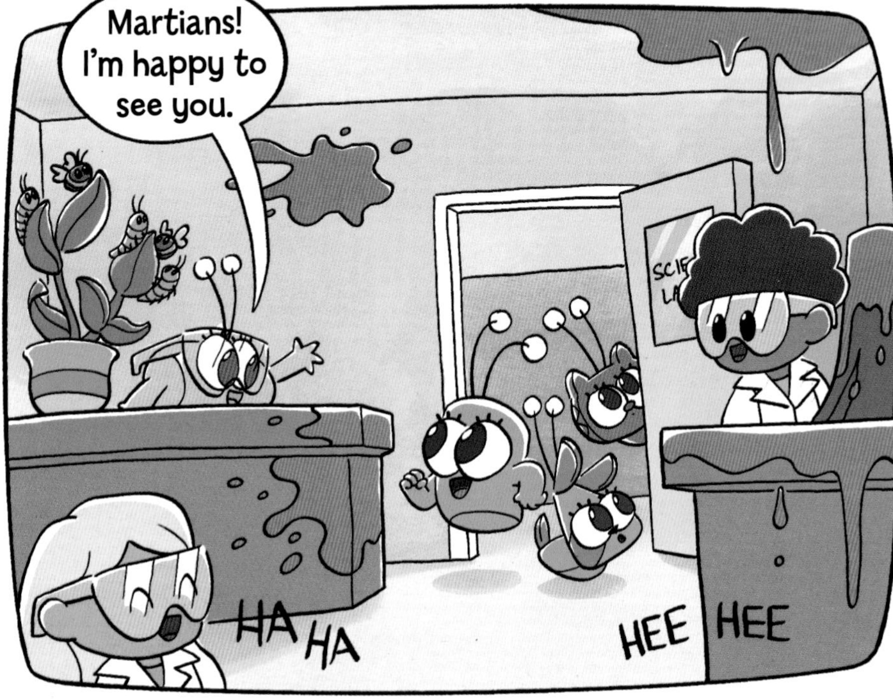
Martians! I'm happy to see you.
SCIE LA
HA HA
HEE HEE

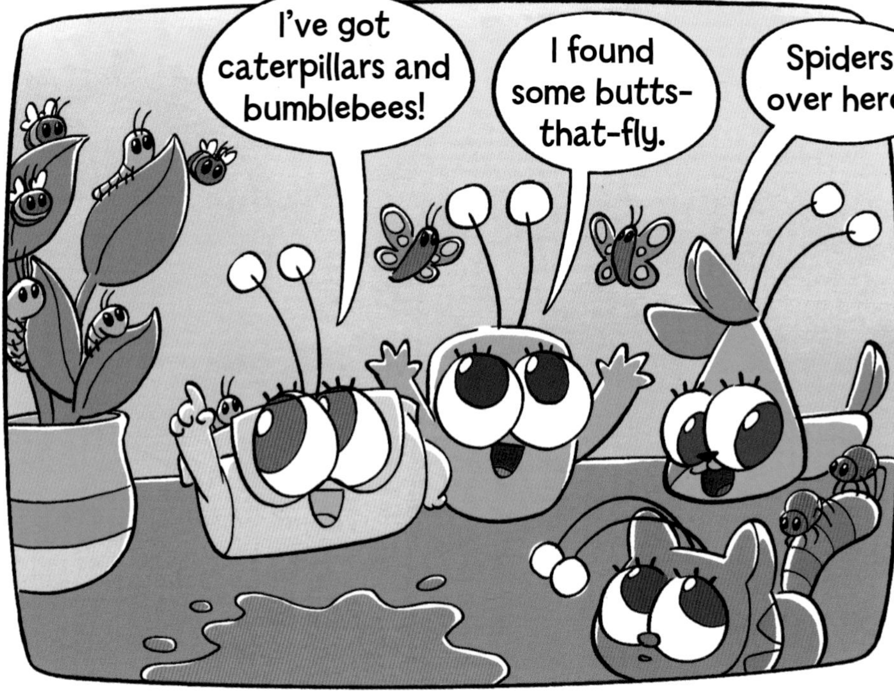
I've got caterpillars and bumblebees!
I found some butts-that-fly.
Spiders over here!

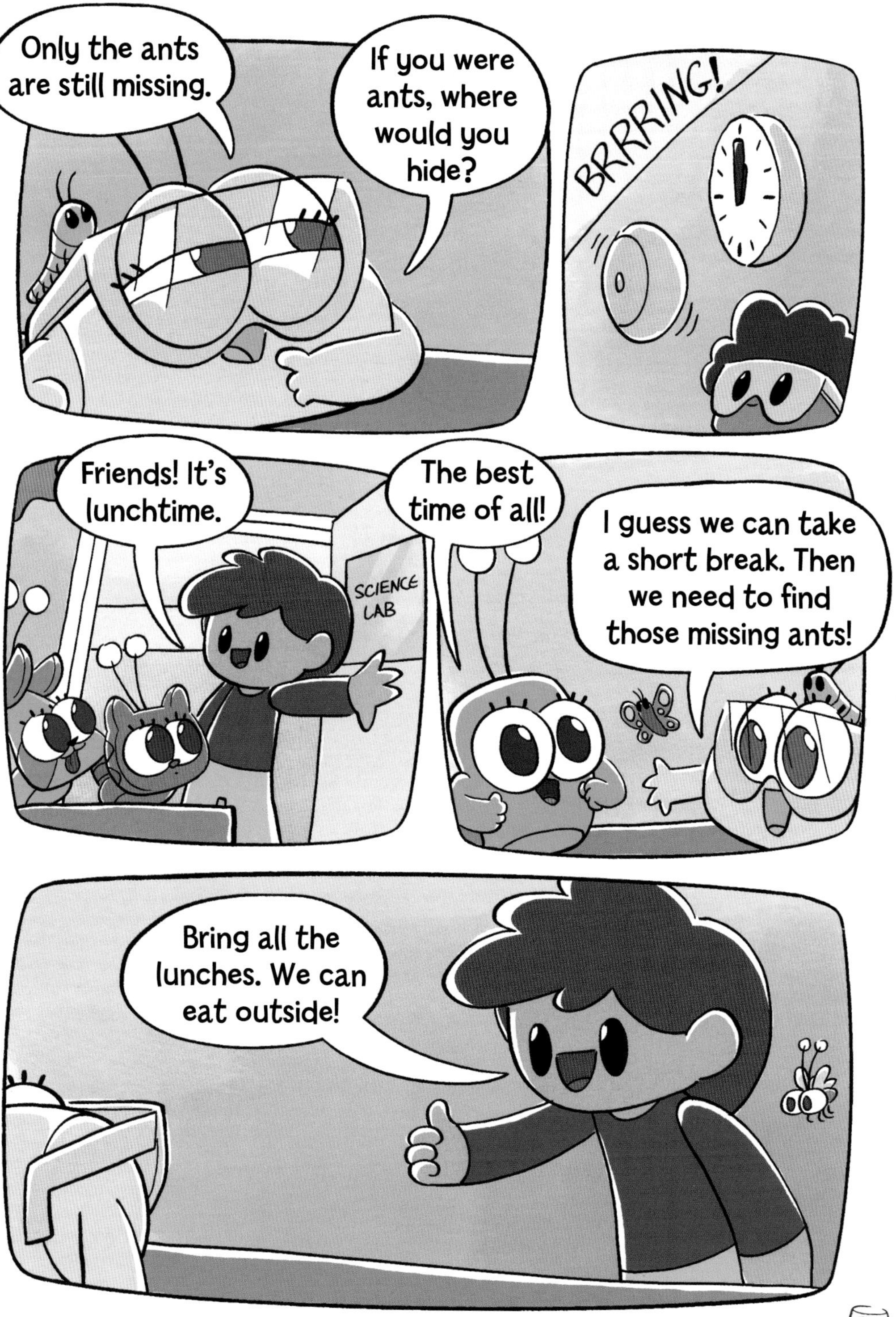
Only the ants are still missing.
If you were ants, where would you hide?
BRRRING!
Friends! It's lunchtime.
SCIENCE LAB
The best time of all!
I guess we can take a short break. Then we need to find those missing ants!
Bring all the lunches. We can eat outside!

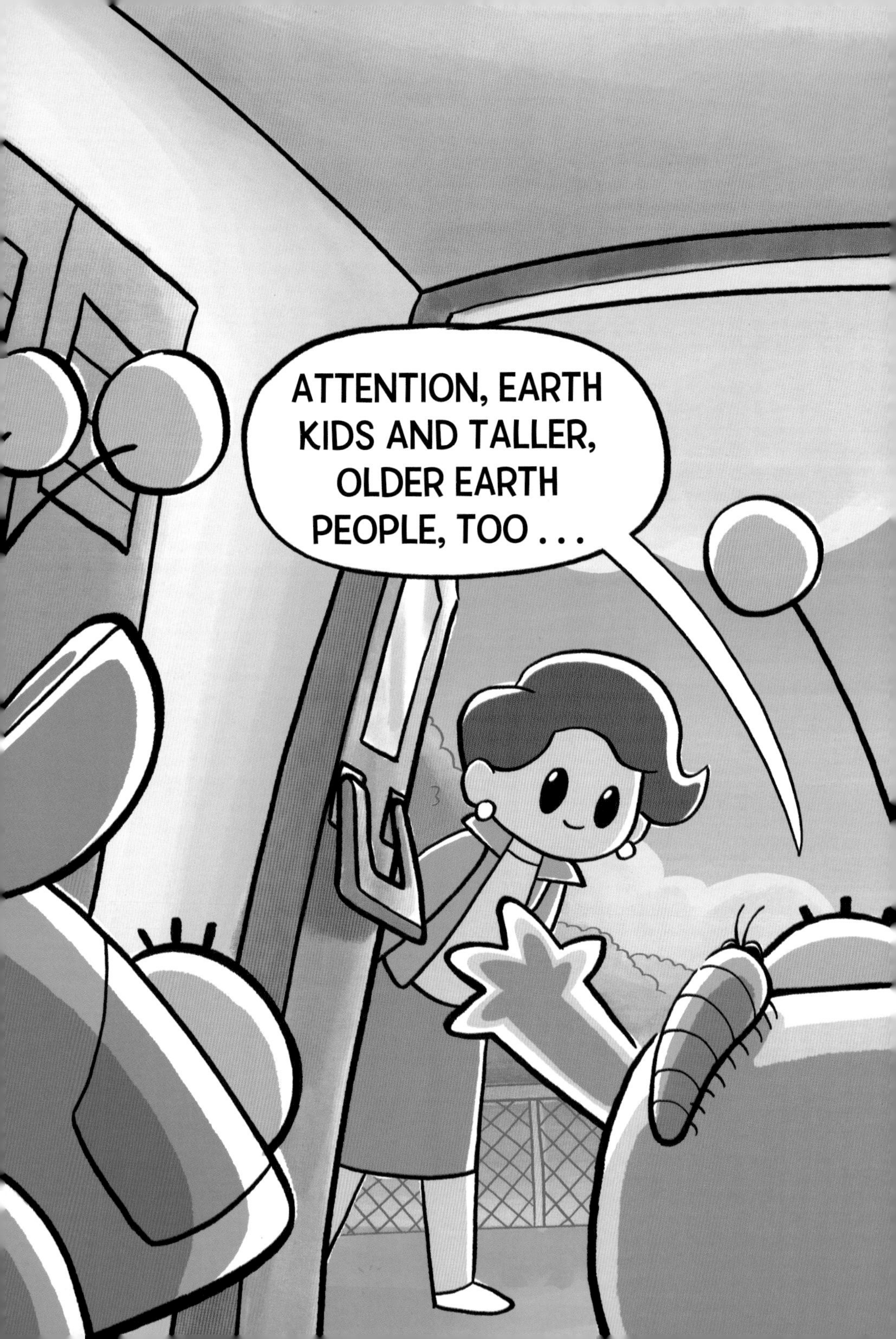
ATTENTION, EARTH KIDS AND TALLER, OLDER EARTH PEOPLE, TOO . . .

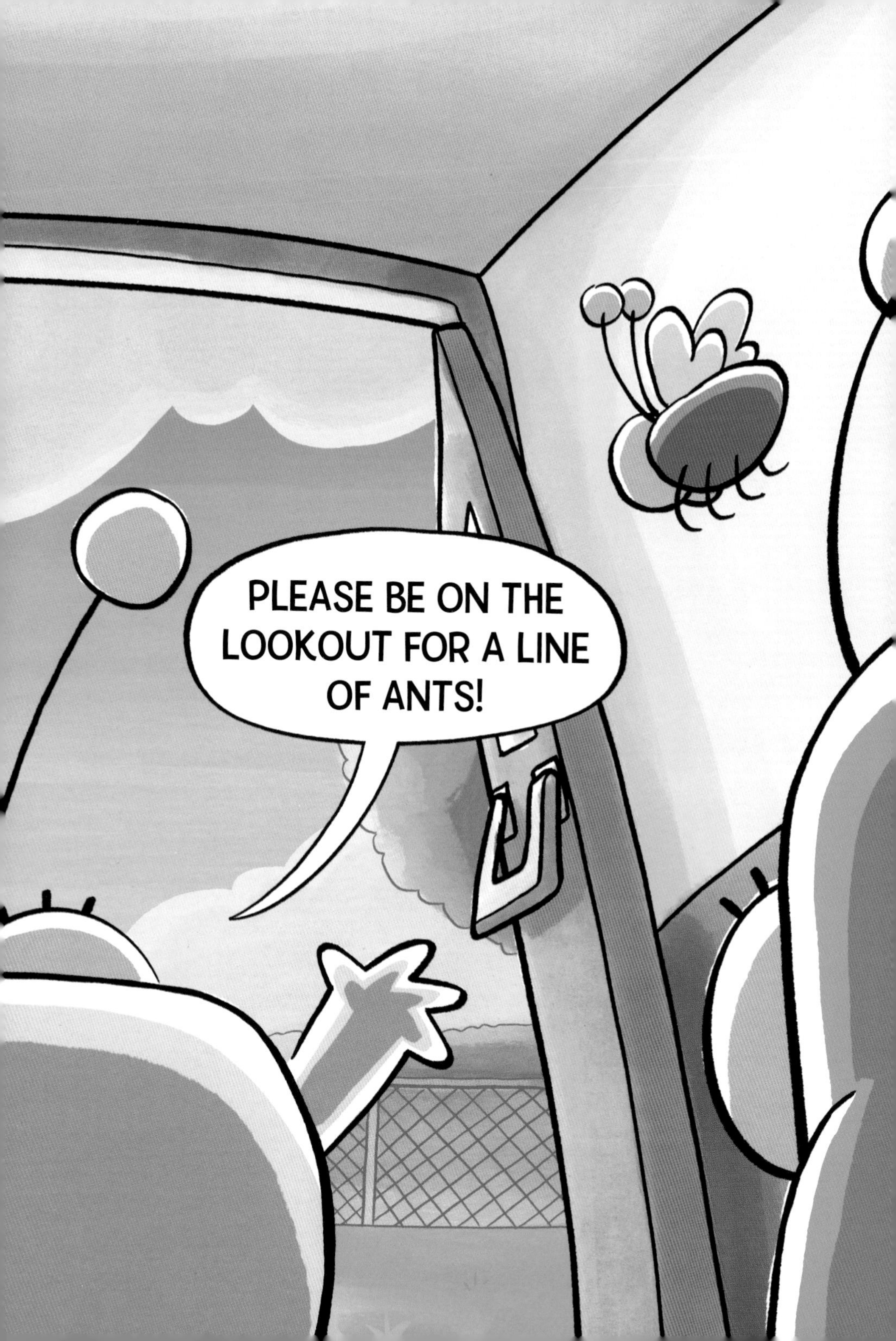
PLEASE BE ON THE LOOKOUT FOR A LINE OF ANTS!

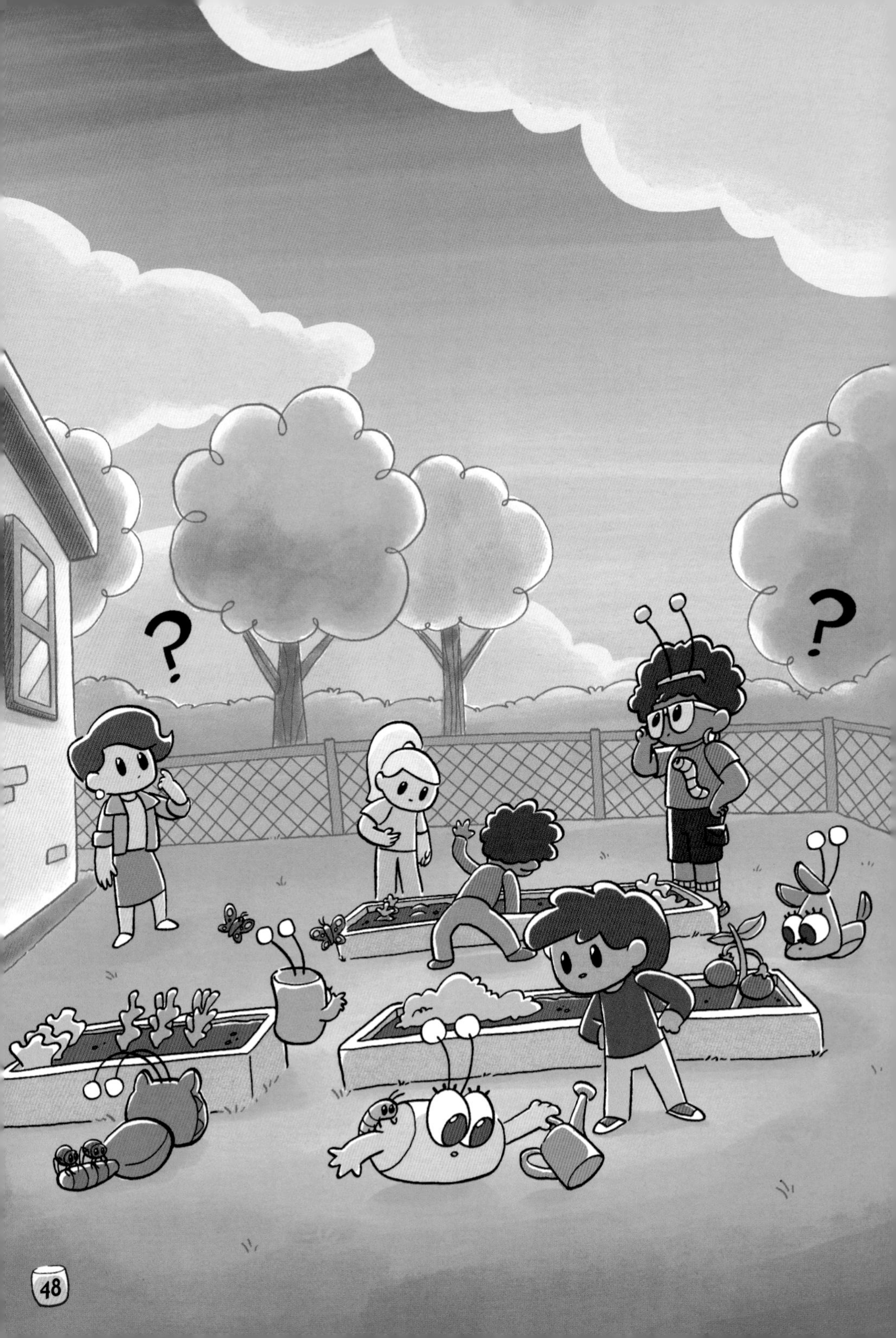
?
?

Chapter 6
Picnic Ant-ics!

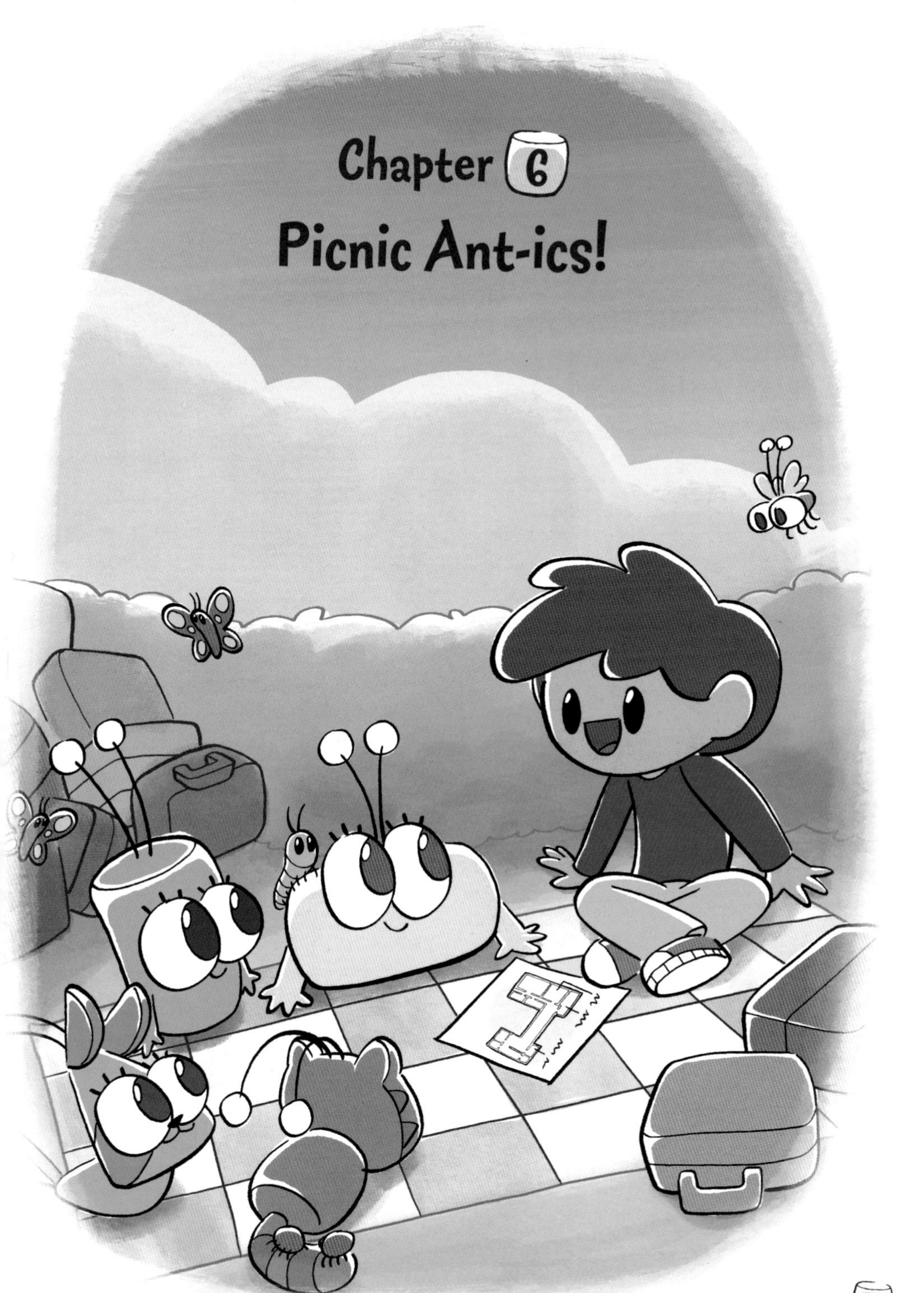

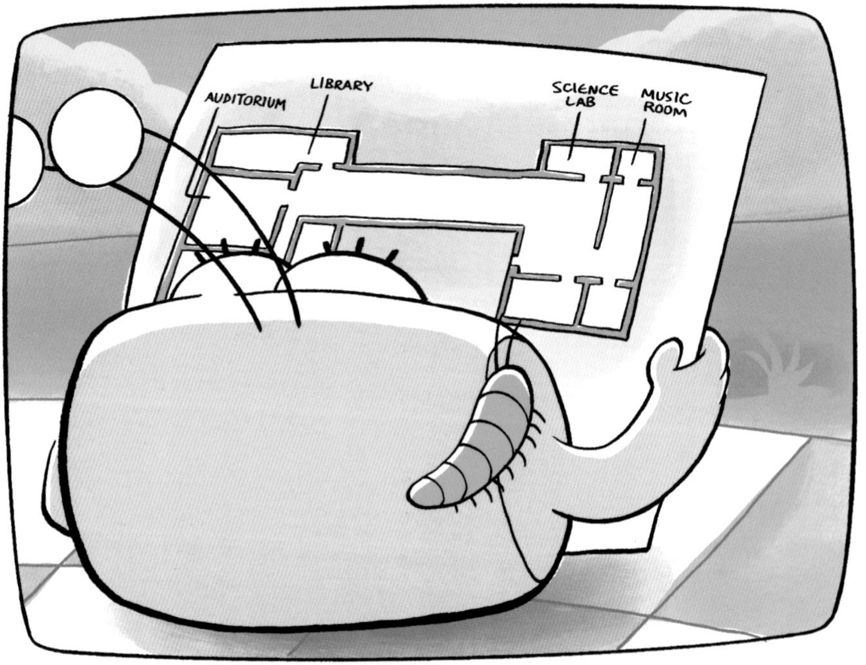
AUDITORIUM
LIBRARY
SCIENCE LAB
MUSIC ROOM

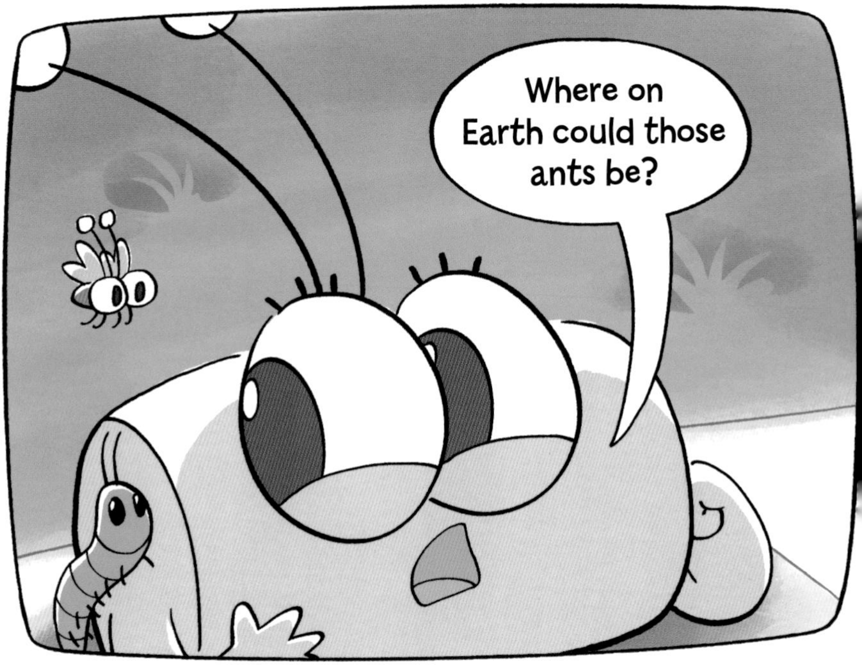
Where on Earth could those ants be?

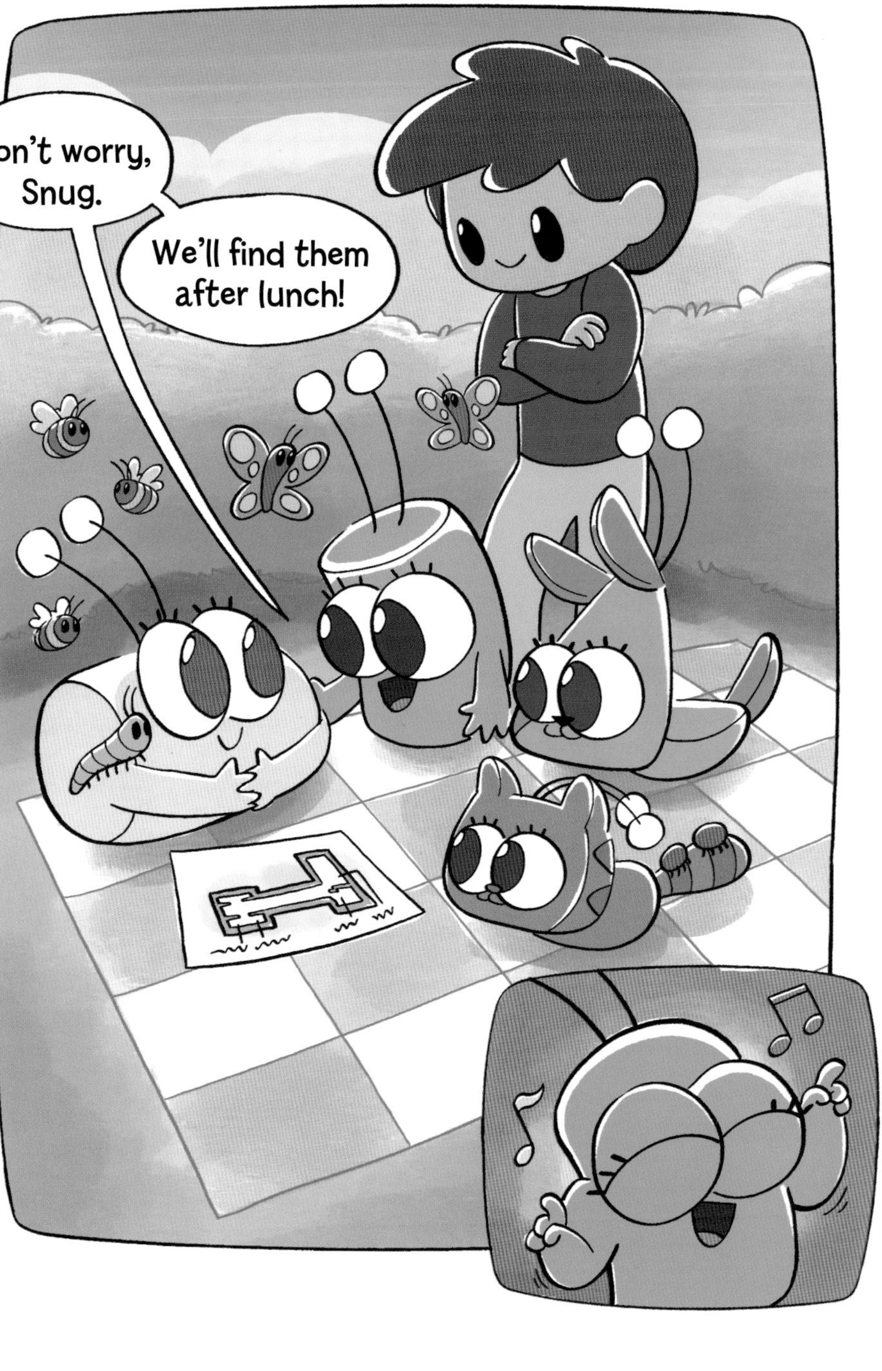
Don't worry, Snug.
We'll find them after lunch!

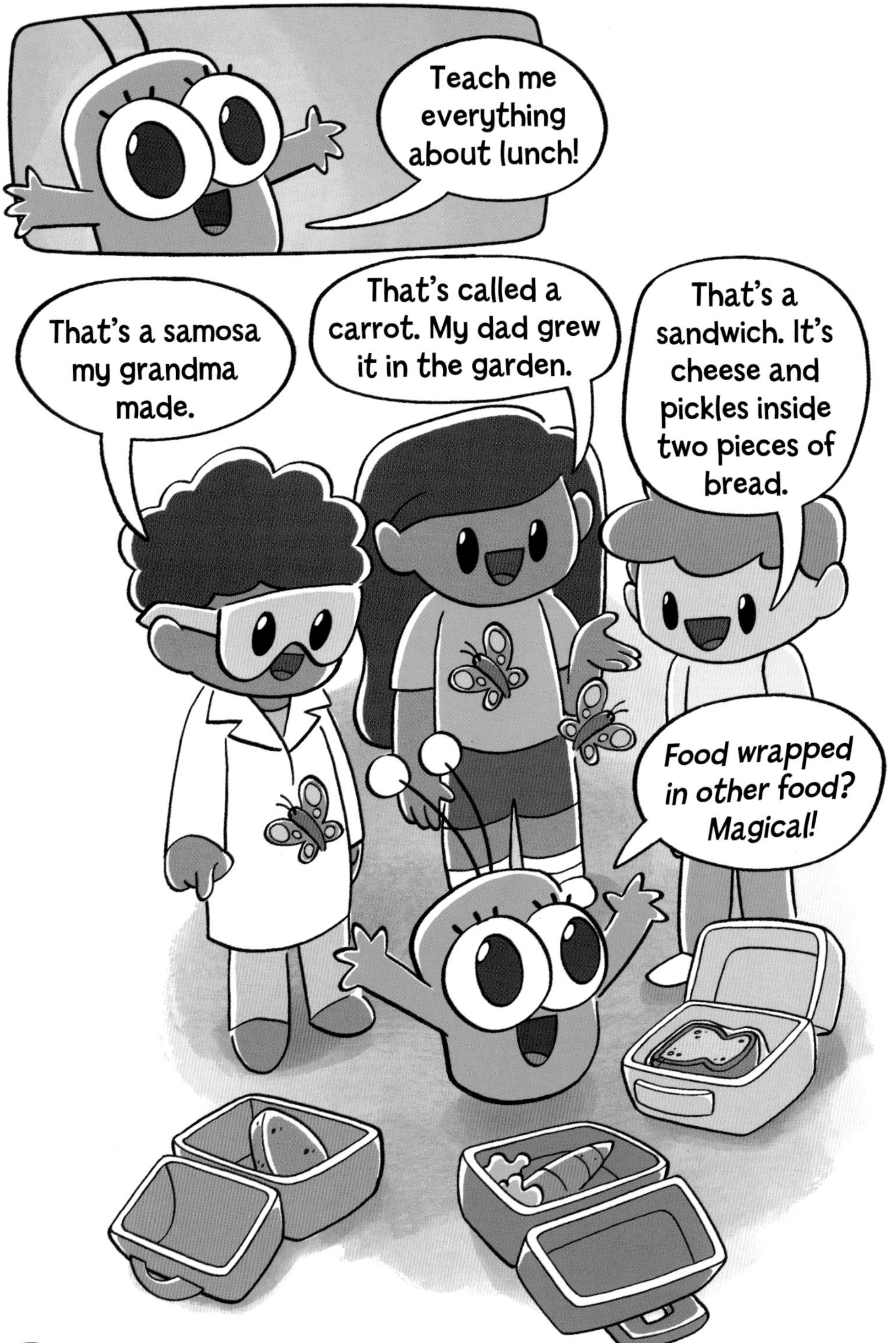
Teach me everything about lunch!
That's a samosa my grandma made.
That's called a carrot. My dad grew it in the garden.
That's a sandwich. It's cheese and pickles inside two pieces of bread.
Food wrapped in other food? Magical!

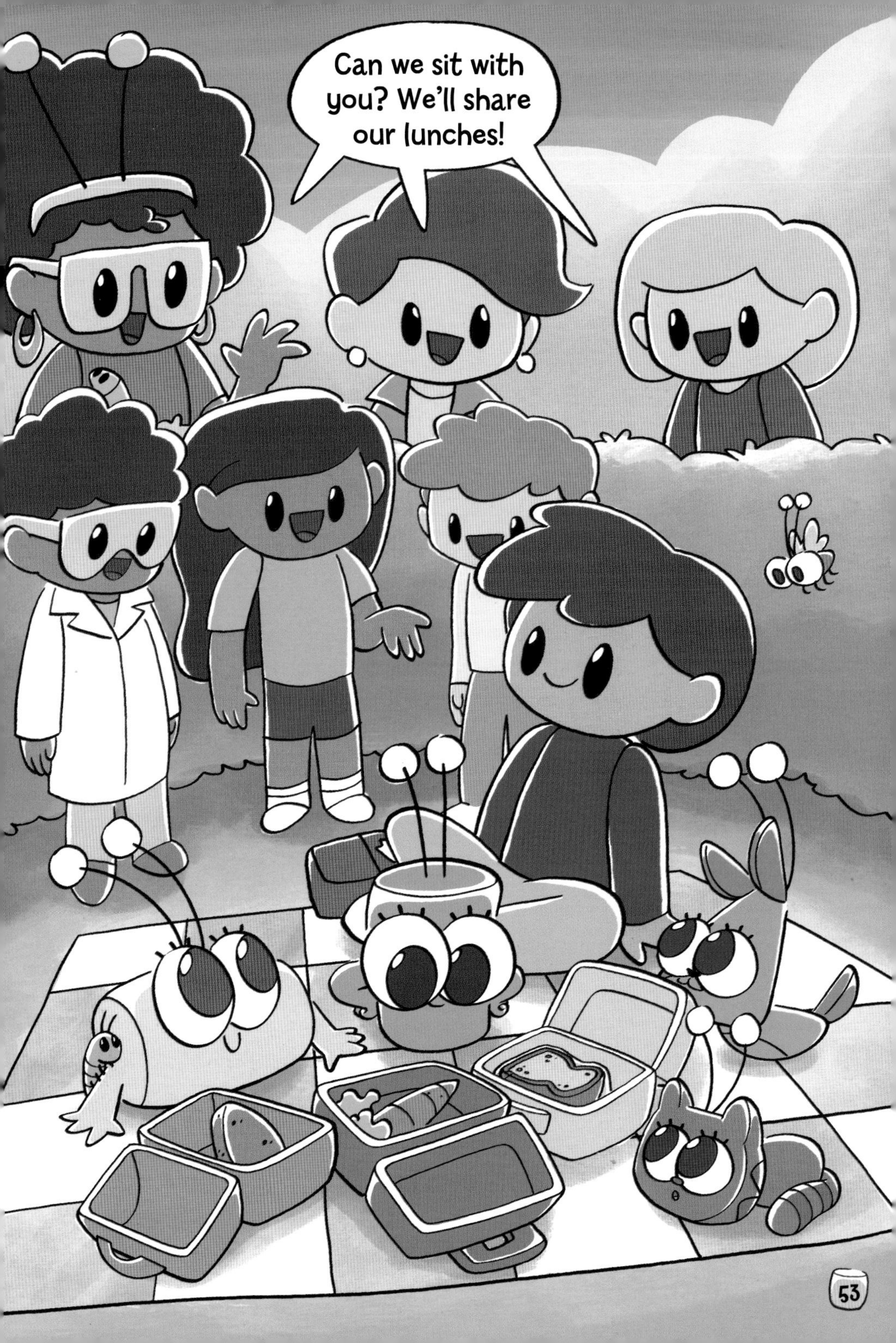
Can we sit with you? We'll share our lunches!

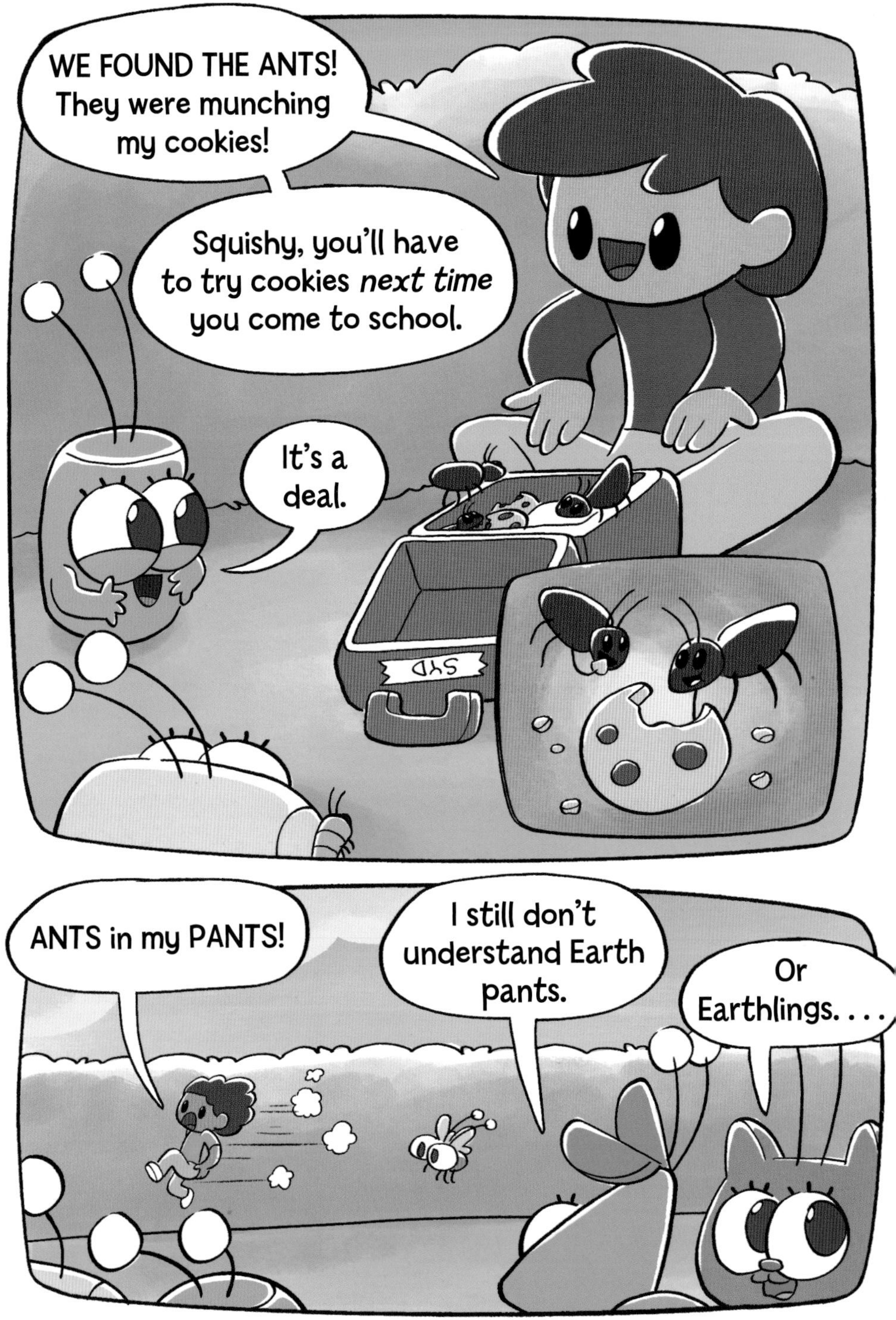
WE FOUND THE ANTS! They were munching my cookies!
Squishy, you'll have to try cookies *next time* you come to school.
It's a deal.
SYD
ANTS in my PANTS!
I still don't understand Earth pants.
Or Earthlings. . . .

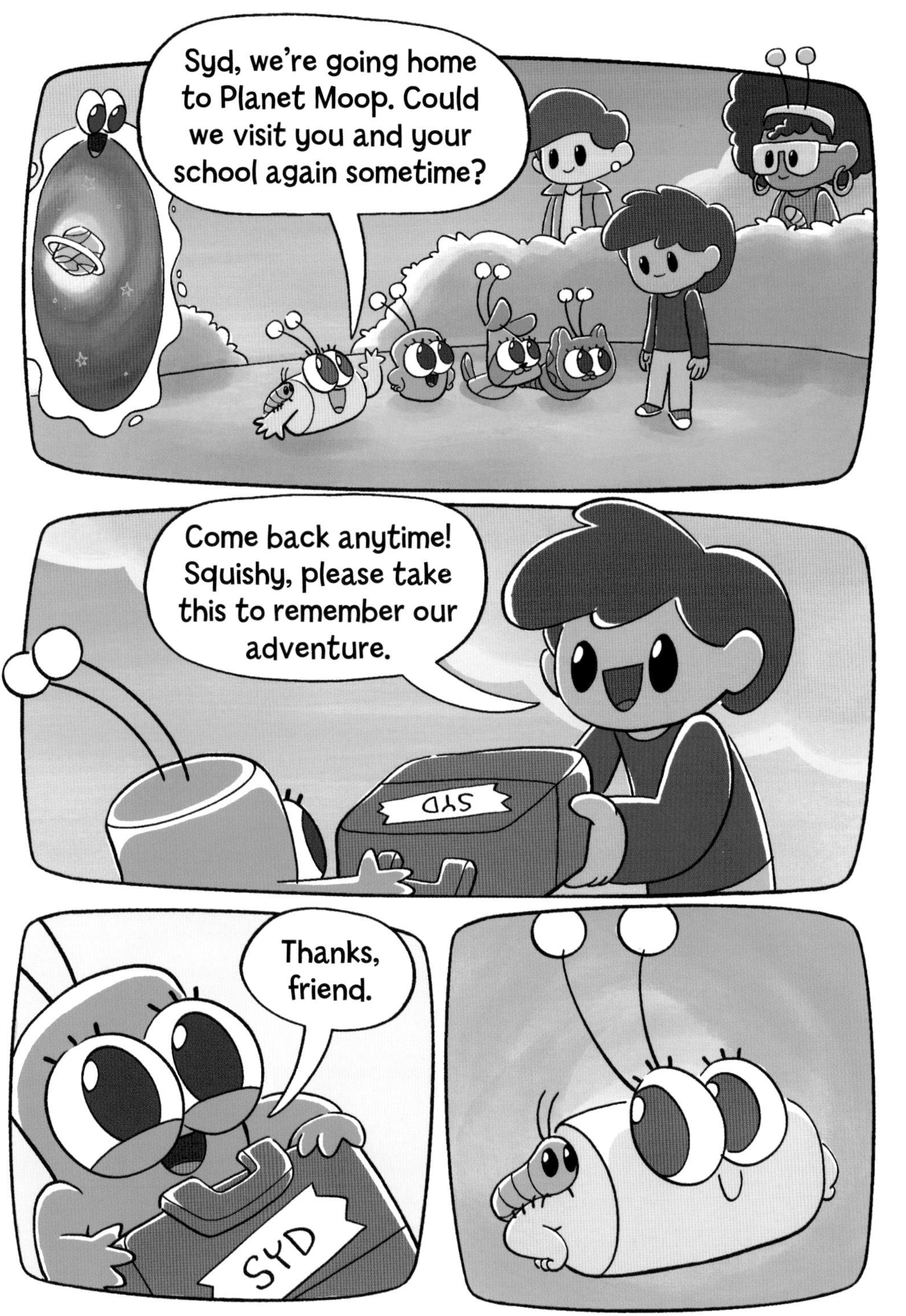
Syd, we're going home to Planet Moop. Could we visit you and your school again sometime?
Come back anytime! Squishy, please take this to remember our adventure.
SYD
Thanks, friend.
SYD

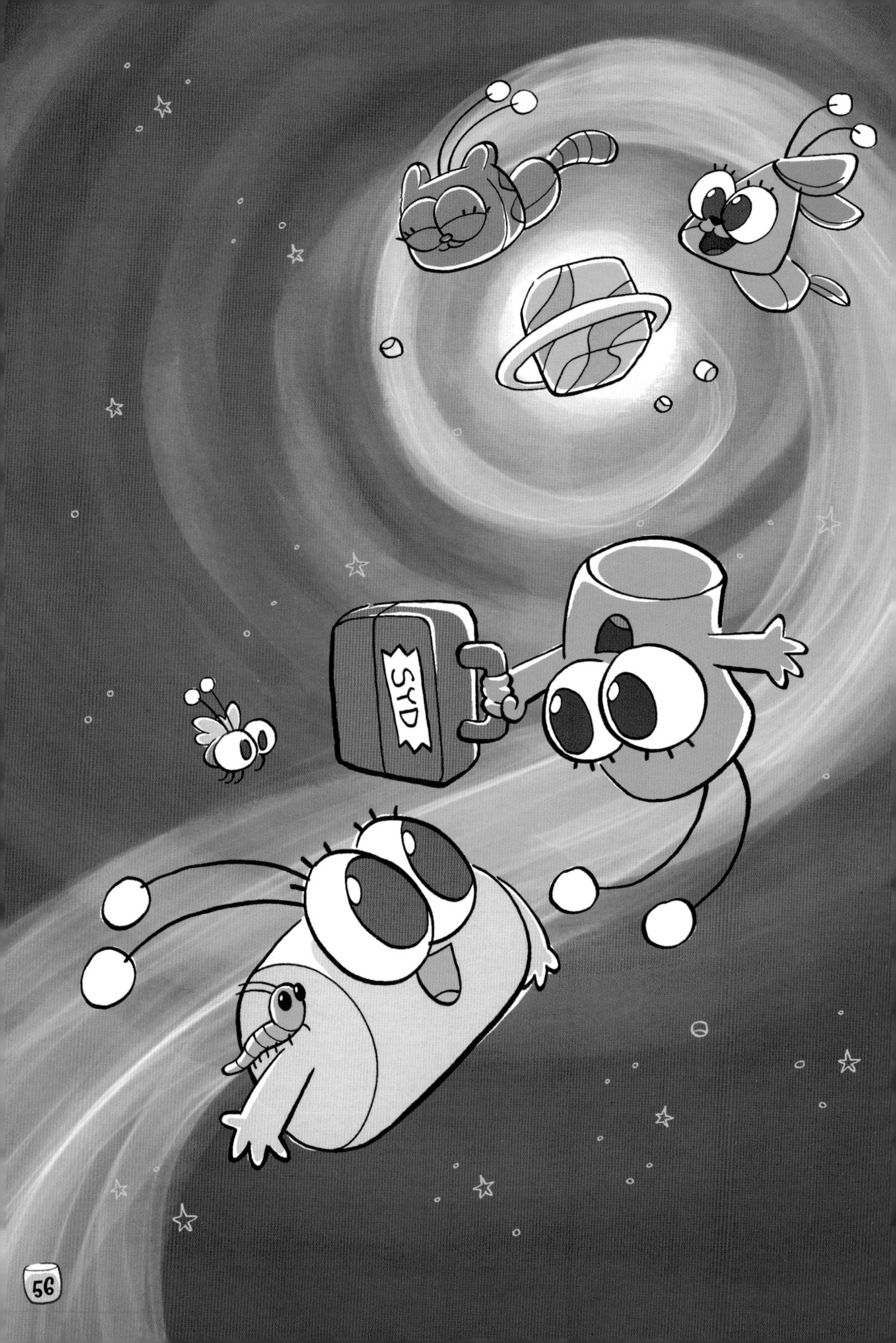
SYD

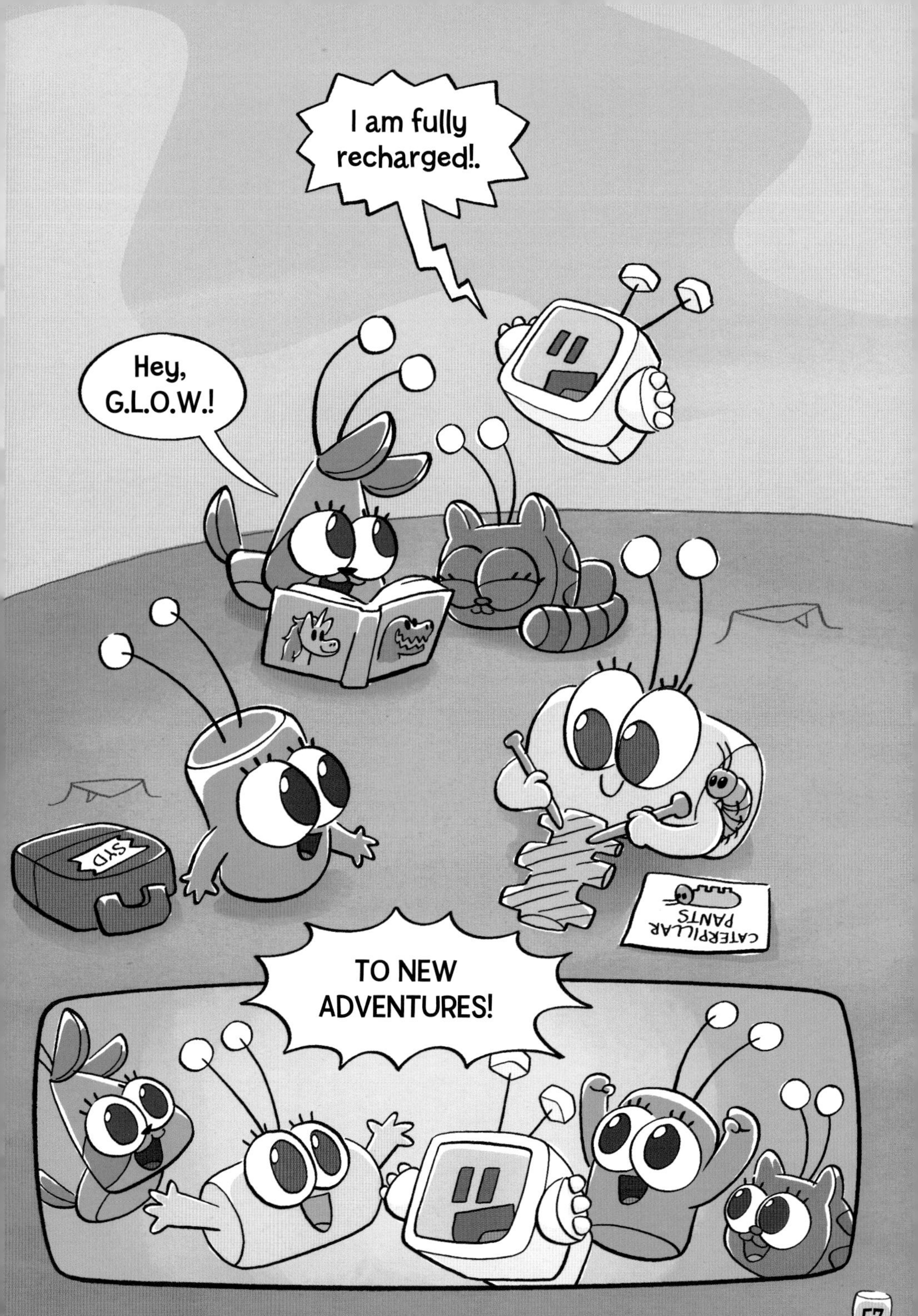
I am fully recharged!.
Hey, G.L.O.W.!
SYD
CATERPILLAR PANTS
TO NEW ADVENTURES!

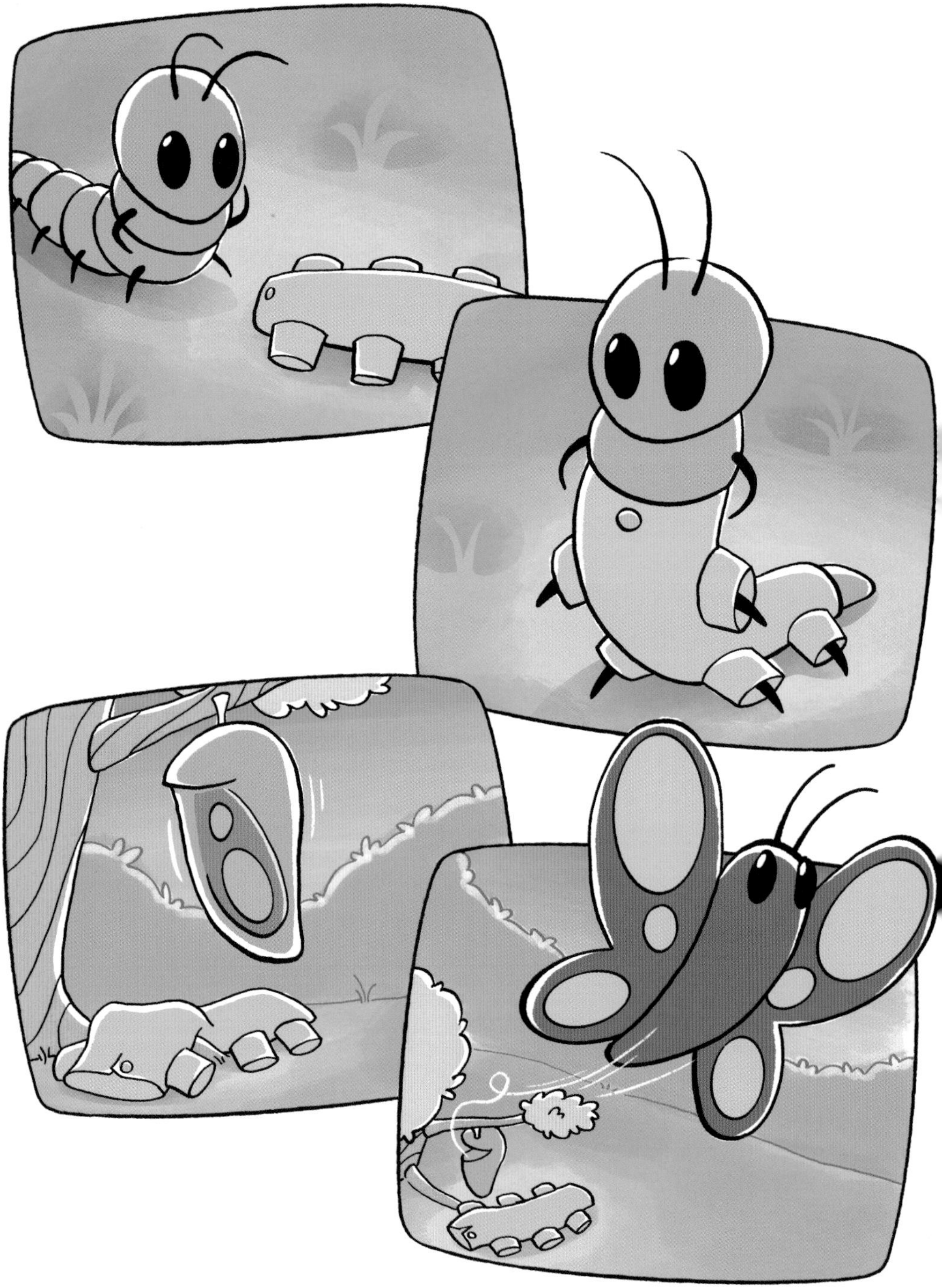

Acknowledgments

Remembering Jeff Hooson
and his love for stories and adventures.

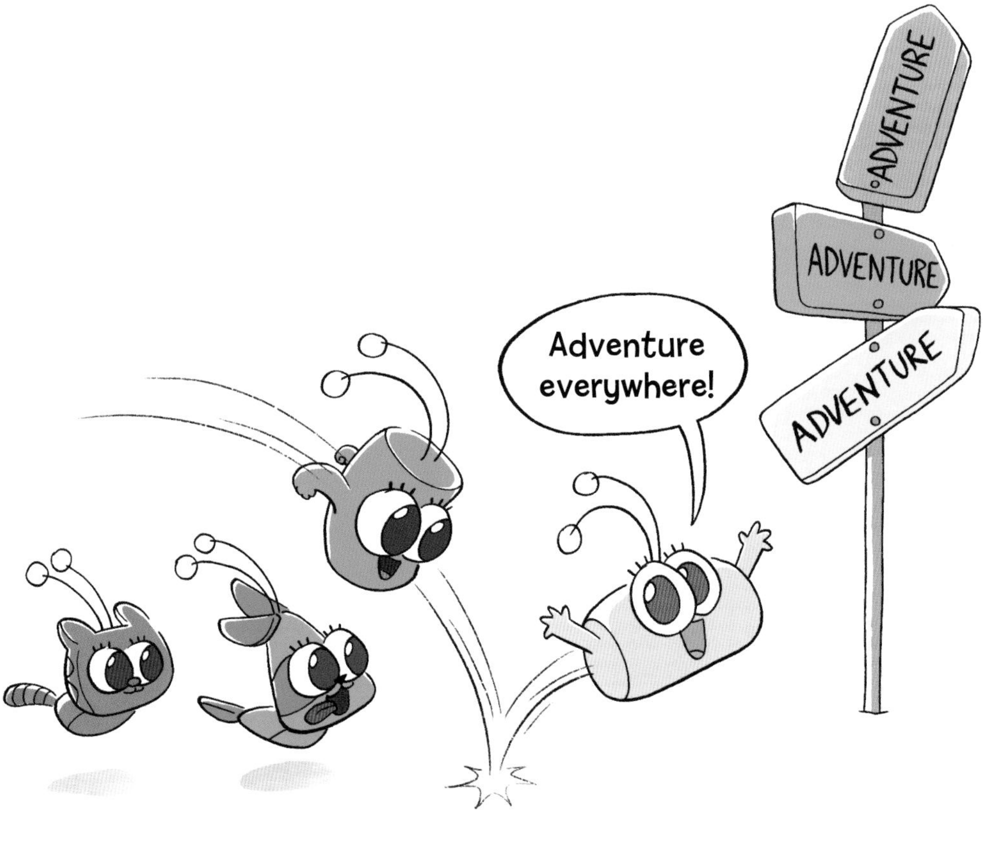
ADVENTURE
ADVENTURE
ADVENTURE
Adventure everywhere!

How to Draw Squishy!

1. Start with a tall, squishy marshmallow shape.

2. Draw Squishy's eyes, arms, and mouth!

3. Add antennae, a tongue, and eye shines.

4. Erase any extra lines, and add color!

Note from Neil: If your drawing of Squishy looks different from the Squishy in this book, that's perfect! It means you've added your own artistic flair and made it one of a kind. It's so much fun to create unique characters.

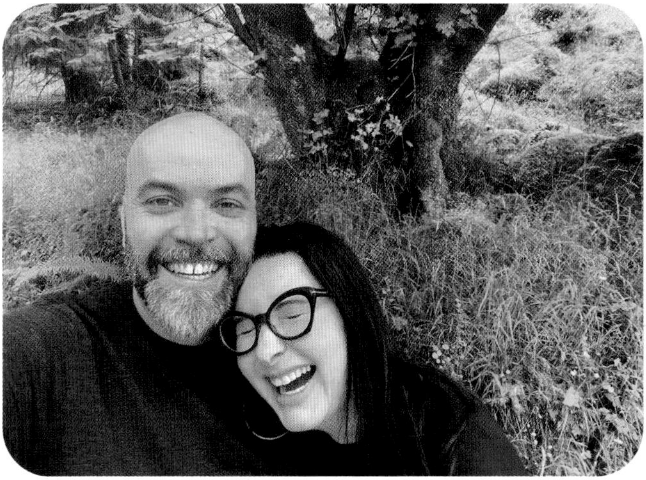

Deanna Kent and **Neil Hooson** are a writer-artist duo in Kelowna, Canada. Deanna loves twinkle lights, Edna Mode, and hiking in the Great Bear Rainforest, where she's obsessed with taking photos of mushrooms, slugs, and other foresty things. Neil is king of his Les Paul guitar, makes killer enchiladas, and dreams of seeing the pyramids one day. He really wants aliens to land in his backyard. By far, their greatest creative challenge is raising four (very busy, very amazing) boys and their giant dog, Hugo.

Visit them on the web at deannaandneil.com.

@DeannaandNeil

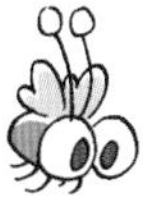

Hide-and-seek, gemstones, and dinosaur bones?
The Marshmallow Martians are about to have the

BEST SLEEPOVER EVER!

Where are you?
That human really loves this game.
Ugh. Can't we play hide-and-snack instead?
Let's keep him happy and hide one last time.
This triangle seems like a good hiding spot.
So many tunnels!
There are pictures on this wall.
It's an ancient comic book!
They're called hieroglyphs.
Fuzz! They are carrying that cat around!

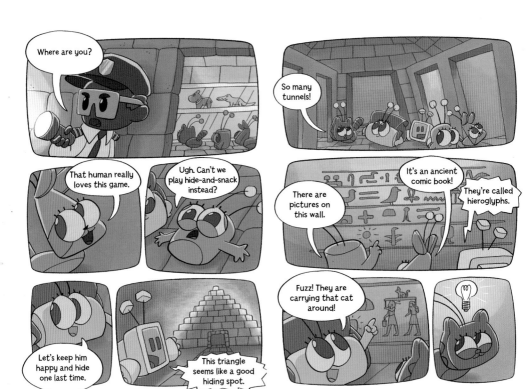

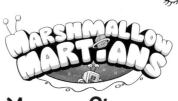